Praise for *Go* **T0152385**

A beautiful and haunting portrait of a marriage that scrambled my thoughts on faith, power, love and sacrifice. This text embodies the act of questioning in a way that is at once startling and affirming. A gorgeous, important book. – Jac Jemc, author of *The Grip of It* and *False Bingo*

God's Wife is an incredible book. Playful and deeply disturbing at the same time, fierce and funny, a romantic comedy and a profound philosophical treatise at the same time—and many, many other things. It's a book like no other I've ever read, a book impossible to pull off. I have no idea how Amanda Michalopoulou did it. – Daniel Kehlmann, author of *Measuring the World*

God's Wife is a stunningly brilliant book. At every turn, it avoids obviousness and cliché. The writing, crisp, clear, clever and compelling. It is a moving love story that unfolds with the rigorous intellectual logic of a piece of first-rate theology, into a vast, beautiful repetitive loop that urges the reader on to make fresh associations and new lines of thought. Highly recommended. – Simon Critchley, author of *The Book of Dead Philosophers*

God's Wife is a novel of marvels—and marvelous, in how splendidly Michalopoulou has conjured and told this story of the longing of a young girl for God, for great love. Her voice is charming and engaging, even though God doesn't always answer her questions. *God's Wife* is an allegorical work that speaks to these troubling times with an unusual voice, with wit and intelligence. – Lynne Tillman, author of *Men and Apparitions*

In Amanda Michalopoulou's wonderfully strange, emphatically beautiful and often very funny new novel, a woman with a hard-earned grasp on quantum physics and complex spiritual doctrine composes a letter to those of us who still live in time (in the windowless room where she writes the word *tomorrow* is "as round and yellow as the moon") about what it is like to live as wife to the All-Powerful. Her experiences with a Husband who reads *Don Quixote* and has eyes as "pure and clear as a dog's," sit at the heart of a brilliant exploration of time and being and the existential wonders and terrors of repetition. I can't recommend it highly enough. – Laird Hunt, author of *In the House in the Dark of the Woods*

GOD'S WIFE

Amanda Michalopoulou

GOD'S WIFE

Translated from the Greek by
Patricia Felisa Barbeito

DALKEY ARCHIVE PRESS

McLean, IL / Dublin

Originally published by Εκδόσεις Καστανιώτη Α.Ε. as Η γυναίκα του Θεού in
2014
Copyright © by Amanda Michalopoulou in 2019
Translation copyright © by Patricia Felisa Barbeito, 2019
First Dalkey Archive edition, 2019.

Photographs in the book interior © 2011 Mary Flanagan,
http://www.maryflanagan.com

Library of Congress Cataloging-in-Publication Data

Names: Michalopoulou, Amanta, 1966- author. | Barbeito, Patricia Felisa,
translator.
Title: God's wife / Amanda Michalopoulou ; translated from the Greek by
Patricia Felisa Barbeito.
Other titles: Gynaika tou theou. English
Description: First Dalkey Archive edition. | McLean, Illinois : Dalkey
Archive Press, 2019. | Translation of: Gynaika tou theou.
Identifiers: LCCN 2019033479 | ISBN 9781628973372 (paperback)
Subjects: LCSH: Spiritual life--Fiction.
Classification: LCC PA5624.I27 G9613 2019 | DDC 889.3/34--dc23
LC record available at https://lccn.loc.gov/2019033479

Co-funded by the Creative Europe Programme
of the European Union

Translation supported by the Kostas and Eleni Ouranis Foundation.
Cover photograph courtesy of Nikos Kessanlis archive.

Dalkey Archive Press
McLean, IL / Dublin

Printed on permanent/durable acid-free paper.
www.dalkeyarchive.com

Acknowledgements

This novel was completed with the support of writing residencies at the Shanghai Writing Program and the Bogliasco Foundation (Liguria Study Center for the Arts and Humanities). The photographs at the beginning of each chapter were taken by Mary Flanagan.

For Dimitris and Klara

TRANSLATOR'S INTRODUCTION

INTERNATIONALLY ACCLAIMED GREEK author, Amanda Michalopoulou's seventh novel, *God's Wife*, was first published in Greece in 2014, during the Greek government-debt crisis. At a time of harsh austerity measures and related humanitarian crises, it is perhaps appropriate that the novel is both austere and turbulent, wry and angst-ridden. This, however, is as far as such an analogy can go, for in this novel Michalopoulou does not directly engage the economic and socio-cultural issues of her homeland as she has done in some of her more historically located novels or collections of short stories. In *God's Wife*, she focuses instead on crises of another, parallel order. And she does so in a way that elaborates on the etymological roots of the word crisis as both judgement and the decisive turning point that ushers in change, for better or worse. Indeed, *God's Wife* is fundamentally about the struggles, compromises, and leaps of faith that are required in any relationship: be it to one's husband, one's God, or one's broader community. These concerns, of course, are directly related to her long-standing focus on what it means to write and exercise one's authority as a woman. They are also evident in her established practice of metafiction, which has systematically taken apart the conventions of narrative in order to open up new ways of imagining. "Is it possible to believe in a woman for whom writing is neither titillation nor entertainment—a woman who simply writes?" asks the narrator. *God's Wife*, equal parts fairy tale, myth, epic poem, experimental novel, feminist tract, and philosophical treatise, tries to provide us with an answer.

"It may sound like a lie: I am His wife." From the novel's very
first line, the narrator captivates us with her laconic directness. In
the same breath, she combines youthful uncertainty and mature
confidence, as she asserts herself ("I am") in a world that dis-
misses her experience as a lie. Like so many of Michalopoulou's,
protagonists, the intimate intensity of her voice lays bare the
often-contradictory impulses that shape who we are. While much
of Michalopoulou's fiction dwells on the trials and tribulations
of female characters articulating the difficult, often contentious
processes of their own self-realization, this narrator's voice is
particularly precarious. Are we reading the ramblings of a mad-
woman? Strange revelations from beyond the grave? The insights
of a saint? Or simply the story of a completely ordinary woman
who gave up her whole world for love, and is now struggling to
come to terms with the multiple layers of who she is?

Ultimately, what helps us anchor this supremely slippery
character is the host of fictional predecessors she calls forth. On
the one hand, she brings to mind the beleaguered captive hero-
ines found in the precursors to the modern psychological novel:
the Pamelas and Clarissas (Richardson), the mad women in the
attic (Brontë) and the quintessential romantic and domestic
narratives they shaped. Like them, she is a fresh-faced, high-
minded innocent yearning for love and self-sacrifice, "the kind
of girl who doesn't dare displease anyone, ever; who thirsts for
constraints." Like them, she suffers trauma, loss, the aggressions
of a sadistic brother, until she is saved from it all by a tall, hand-
some stranger with luminous eyes and a kingdom all of His
own. But the story does not end there. The narrator's initial
meekness is soon tinged with doubt and defiance as the utopia
of domesticity is transformed into a struggle with ennui and a
battle of wills, and she begins to resemble some of the proto-her-
oines of the feminist novel. Wavering between self-denial and
an intense desire to know, God's wife is, in fact, very much like
the defiant protagonist of the influential Gothic short story by
Charlotte Perkins Gilman "The Yellow Wallpaper" (clearly an
important intertext for Michalopoulou). With the pencil she
has hidden in her vagina (and its nod to both Hélène Cixous and

Carolee Schneemann), she writes in secret, notwithstanding her husband's express prohibition, seeking to tear off the pattern of silence that He has imposed on her. Trapped in a story in which she has been hitherto complicit, she tries repeatedly to escape, to rewrite it, but her task is exceptionally difficult: her husband is God Himself.

Therein lies the central conceit of Michalopoulou's novel, for the story of the narrator's travels and travails with her enigmatic and taciturn husband opens out into a nuanced and oftentimes wryly humorous meditation on creativity and creation, reality and imagination, freedom and faith, spirituality and physicality, indeed the very nature of truth and love. What ties all these themes together, of course, in typical Michalopoulou fashion, is the novel's sustained, self-conscious attention to the workings of fiction. It is the very foundation of the couple's relationship—what else, besides fiction, could bring these two together?—but it is also what tears them apart. God abhors what reminds Him of His own (failed) creation, and when He finds His wife writing, we know that things can no longer remain as they are. Indeed, the novel is built around a vertiginous, multilayered complex of intertextual reference, from the Dante-esque journey through hell, purgatory and heaven that shape the novel's chapters, to the plethora of references—from Gilgamesh and the Marquis de Sade to Schelling and Simone Weil—that provide fodder for the couple's debates. This ballooning web of intertexts, the gleeful playfulness with which they proliferate both within and beyond the text, models an ethos of writing as a dialogic borrowing or signifyin' (in Henry Louis Gates's definition of the word). Not only, for example, do the narrator and her husband occasionally echo the words of their favorite fictional characters, but the text itself repeatedly calls attention to its own collaborative foundations: "One of my sentences will spring to mind as if it were yours. You will not be wrong: we created it together." The freedom and challenge posed by this mandate to create and re-create the text "together" was one of the great pleasures I found in its translation.

Like many of Michalopoulou protagonists, God's wife is far from home and suffering from nostalgia. Confined to the seamless perfection and monotony of God's kingdom, she is consumed with longing for the worn, imperfect world she has left behind. Her writing, her creation of narrative, is driven by the doomed desire for all she has lost, her home and the impossible fantasy of the happy family, as well as "smells, tastes, the friction of bodies." Her nostalgia recalls what theorist Svetlana Boym in her 2002 book, *The Future of Nostalgia,* described as a "reflective" practice that weds "longing to critical thinking" and represents a "strategy of survival, a way of making sense of the impossibility of homecoming." Given Michalopoulou's resistance in her work to an obvious Greekness or local color in order to emphasize, as she has stated in interviews, "what it means to be human and function in the world" and the "existential" dimensions of the recent Greek crisis, it is interesting to note that Boym describes reflective nostalgia as part of "off-modern" and "eccentric" traditions, "often considered marginal or provincial with respect to the cultural mainstream, from eastern Europe to Latin America" that critique the "deterministic narrative of twentieth-century history." The wife, marginal and eccentric as she is to the absolute power that is God, insists on answers, truth, purpose, a book of her own. God, surrounded by his incomprehensible, mumbling angels, evades, refuses, denies, punishes. If "in the beginning was the Word, and the Word was God," what happens when that word turns out to be empty, a lie? "My greatest fear is that you do not exist," writes the narrator to the reader she insists on addressing directly, "I'm also afraid that perhaps I don't exist." Yet all she can do to assuage these fears is to keep on writing. And the more she writes, the more God seems to withdraw from her so that in the end, He stands for the sublime indifference, the echoing emptiness that drives the desire to create.

Near the end of the novel, the narrator finds herself in a prison, both a heaven and hell, of her own making: "It may sound like a lie: I am trapped in the Book . . . In here, I do as I like with words. When I can no longer stand the stillness, my mind dives onto the page from a great height and I am undone." The Dominican-American author, Junot Diaz has said that novelists are akin to dictators in that they both allow only one person to speak: "We all dream dreams of unity, of purity; we all dream that there's an authoritative voice out there that will explain things, including ourselves. If it wasn't for our longing for these things, I doubt the novel or the short story would exist in its current form." Michalopoulou, like her narrator, dives into the pages of the novel from the headiest pinnacles of the literary tradition and what comes undone in these "waves of paper," as the narrator calls them, is the very illusion of purity, unity, and authority that the novel enshrines. Indeed, the greatest achievement of this artful novel may very well be what it does to us as readers: it beckons us in, seduces us with tantalizing glimpses of hidden truths, only to tease us, frustrate us, send us on our way: "Don't let me keep you . . . I release you, Reader, with my blessing." Like the narrator, we are left caught in the book, living between the lines, wandering among the black and white of pages that are ultimately a love letter to the possibilities and limits of the novel itself.

Patricia Felisa Barbeito

The problem's climbing the sycamore
to see if maybe the Lord is going by.
Alas I'm no treecreeper,
and even on tiptoes I've never seen Him.

Eugenio Montale
(trans. William Arrowsmith)

INFERNO

It is centuries since I believed in you.
But today my need of you has come back (. . .)
O God, I want to sit on your knees
On the all-too-big throne of Heaven,
And fall asleep with my hands tangled in your grey beard.

Katherine Mansfield, "To God the Father"

It may sound like a lie: I am His wife. We married ages ago. He asked for my hand and I said yes. Sometimes, not even I can quite believe all the things I have lived, first without Him, then by His side. I never imagined my life like this.

I'm writing these pages to tell you my story. I could just as easily say that it's to keep the promise I made to my brother. I should have written him off, but you know how it is: people forget and no matter how far they go, the day always comes when they long for home. But this is not for my brother. Nor am I writing out of a need for solidarity exactly. To care, to be truly human, one must live among other people. What brings us close is the knowledge of a shared, a common fate. I have forgotten the meaning of the most basic things: a slap in the face; sewing back a button hanging by its thread; enclosing arms offering comfort.

I have yet to give any thought to what you'll make of this letter. The only thing that matters is the conviction that you are listening. Having lived for so long by the side of Him who created All from Nothing, I am finally creating something of my own. I am creating you. Who are you? I don't care—be whoever you want to be, so long as you seem real enough for me to talk to. The belief that I'm talking to another human being may just save me. Ironic, right? People turn to God for salvation, but I'm turning to you. My biggest fear is that you don't really exist; that perhaps, defeated by doubt, I'll leave these pages half-written and my story—my terrible story—untold.

I also fear that perhaps life is over there—behind the Shelf, that I'm the one who doesn't really exist. I don't know how else to put it, but I feel like an imaginary woman who took a plunge into the sea of eternity and now doesn't remember how to pull herself back onto the firm shore of the present. At times I ask myself: Am I really here? Is this life of mine really life? And then I say to myself: Are you crazy? You're His wife! And when that isn't enough to convince me, I prick myself with a pin. Or I write.

If I exist and you exist and you accept that He exists, then we're off to a good start. If you believe that He's at His most distant when you most need Him, that He is both inscrutable and inaccessible, then you're on the right track. And you will have reason to listen to my story. Your story.

WHEN I WAS little, I used to draw in the kitchen. Our Formica table was flaking, and I loved picking at its curling surface. It's fun to pick at something that is falling apart. I'd hide the gashes under my notebook. "Someone's been picking at the Formica again!" Mother would grumble.

In the evenings, while she cooked, I'd sit beside her, drawing. There was always a roll of paper stacked away in the kitchen. I'd lay it flat on the table to draw my picture of the day. Slicing straight across with scissors, Mother would cut off the sheet, crumple it into a ball, and throw it in the garbage can. Then, she'd fasten the roll with an elastic band and put it back in its place. Every night, I drew a picture on the paper. I learned to throw it away by myself and then wrap the elastic band around the roll.

One day, Mother leaned over my shoulder, "What are you drawing?"

"God," I replied.

"But we don't know what God looks like."

"We'll find out soon enough."

She used to tell this story all the time. She also kept the drawing. Mother never beat around the bush and was known far and wide for her entertaining yet simple stories. People like their stories simple, without verbosity or pedantry. The story about my drawing of God was a success. As far as I remember, so was the drawing. My God was a weary-looking man. With firm strokes of my pencil, I'd given Him a very fine beard. He was posed as if at rest, a bouquet of flowers in His hands. A wedding? No, I enjoyed drawing flowers. I did not yet fantasize about weddings and bouquets. It's impossible to imagine something truly distant.

Funnily enough, I dressed up as a nun for carnival that year. Mother borrowed the costume from a family friend and raised the hem so I wouldn't trip over it. The veil was grey poplin with a white ribbon to hold back my hair. During recess, I blessed the girls in my class and urged them to confess. In place of communion bread, I gave them pieces of the sesame pretzel I'd taken to school for a snack. Later, at the party, the boys sought me out and asked me to pray to God to help them win their war against the older boys. I knelt down: "God doesn't want anyone to win," I whispered. "He wants peace." This frightened the boys. They abandoned their war and played soccer instead.

Mother's friend did not ask for her costume back. When it rained, I'd wear my veil and hear my older brother's confession. He aspired, he said, to end up in maximum security prison. Eyes glittering, he described the terrible things he'd done. Sometimes, he would snarl rather than speak. I stopped playing that game with him.

Home alone, I would don the veil and pray for my salvation. I didn't use that word; I simply wished my life were different. It wasn't a bad life, just very boring. Once, I dreamed it was the end of the world. The earth flooded, the skies darkened, and muddy water rose everywhere, threatening to drown us. Kneeling down, I prayed. "I believe in One God the Father Almighty, maker of heaven and earth, and of all things visible and invisible." The loose floorboard in front of my bed caved in, a torrent of light gushing from the depths beneath. It was Him: He had no face, only a distended mouth—like a plastic donut float—that hovered in the air and said, "Faith is your salvation."

Once awake, I continued daydreaming: God and I, surfing on the loose floorboard. Riding the cresting waves, soaring to the skies. Aloft there, I got Him to find and save all my loved ones. We sat around a cloud table eating paradise soup. With His enormous mouth, He gulped down more soup than all the rest of us put together.

I THINK BACK on that childhood dream of mine, about God and I teetering on the surf-board, slaloming higher and higher. I suppose everyone dreams about the sky, its vastness, its mystery. We humans are not only creatures of action, but also of sensibility, of imagination.

Forgive me for speaking like this. I'm not trying to be clever. I'm only trying to understand what brought me here: was it my imagination or the whims of chance? In my youth, I took things as they came. Without thinking too much about them, worrying about neither the little things nor life's larger questions. Like a sleepwalker, I went wherever I was led. Perhaps you've heard people talk about the fall from the sublime world of ideas to the profane world of matter? I belonged to neither of those worlds. My life still strolled along childhood's careless paths: tripping on air, I was taking a tailspin into absurdity and emptiness. But perhaps I'm exaggerating. Or suffering from that common middle-age affliction: bitterness.

I'm writing to you in the small, windowless laundry room. I used to iron and sew in here. I couldn't stand inactivity—local code for spirituality, it turns out—so I used to sew dresses and skirts; I even knit cardigans. When I was bored, I would prick my fingertips and watch the oozing blood. That is what I used to do with my hands before I discovered reading and writing. Now, I lock myself in here to write to you. So long as I write, I have purpose. I don't need the evidence of blood.

I am an individual. Like you. This statement probably sounds banal to you, but when I repeat it to myself I always end up in tears. I wipe my eyes, pick up my pencil. To me, it is the most beautiful, the most useful of objects. Like Him, it creates something out of nothing.

I don't really have a plan. At first, I thought that writing to you would be like starting a game of Solitaire: I would cut, I would deal, I would pick up cards. In mathematical jargon, the game would be called an exercise in chance probability. But what use to me are the theory of probability and the mysteries of statistics? Here, I'm no longer the best student in class, nor am I studying to get good grades—there are no grades to be had. I pass the time drawing diagrams, trying to make sense of past events. My relationship with time has been turned upside down, inside out, so please forgive this fragmented back and forth.

My life came undone before I met Him, when my parents were killed in . . . No. This card—the Joker of Despair—I'll save for later. God forbid your attention should hinge on pity. One thing I detest is people who gather around to shed crocodile tears. No, my situation is different. If I dared call things by name, I would say that solitude has shattered me; that I have been crushed by the weight of what I know. In short, I don't know whether I am doing this for me or for you. Who cares? We both have something to gain: you, the Truth, and I, Revelation.

So, I begin with a loaded deck. The very first card I'll show you is how I met Him.

I was finishing high school. One evening, on our way home from afterschool tutoring, my brother announced he was going to take me to a remote spot and tie me to a tree. We lived in town, but we used to walk to afterschool on a road that led into the countryside. It wound around a desolate hill (when I say "desolate," my mind travels back to the world before God, before the creation of hills. It is an annoying habit: whenever I use the adjective "desolate" it takes me back to the time when God was by Himself—ontologically, cosmically alone—before anything else, outside God, had a name).

We started horsing around as soon as we arrived at the hill. Kicking up dirt with our shoes, whistling, tossing our backpacks in the air. We could hear the faraway thrum of car engines. Pretending they were not cars, but chainsaws slicing through tree trunks in the depths of a forest, we made up stories about those imaginary woods. I believed those stories, like I believed in God emerging from beneath the loose floorboard in my bedroom. By human standards, my mind was a bit off. Ideas popped into my head without encountering the slightest resistance. I readily believed things that made others laugh out loud.

My brother had rope with him. I thought it was another of his inventions, a new game of torture. So I let him tie me up. His grasp was strong, his hands leaden on me. "Too tight?" he asked insincerely. "My instructions were to bring you here and tell you not to be scared. They're coming to take you," he added, earnestly this time. Receding down the hill until he was a mere speck on the winding path, he turned towards me. Making a funnel with his hands, he yelled: "Promise that you'll come back, that you'll tell me what it's like!"

"I promise," I replied at the top of my lungs. This was how the game was played, I thought.

It started to rain. I remember dogs howling in the dark, the moon livid like a corpse's face. I could no longer hear cars. The rain fell furiously, strong gusts carving a lattice of streams in the dirt. My clothes clung heavily to me, smelling of Auntie's dirty washcloths. (My aunt had taken care of us after my parents died. She was devout, and insisted that I frequently make the sign of the cross. But she suffered from arthritis and had trouble walking. She would not be climbing up the hill to save me.)

I cried, shrieked, prayed to the blessed Virgin for mercy. Tied to the tree, I fell asleep.

"I READILY BELIEVED things that made others laugh out loud."

Re-reading yesterday's sentence, I worry that you will think me mad. Since I lost the ability to beguile along with the ability to tell stories, the danger is twice as great. Is it possible to believe in a woman for whom writing is neither titillation nor entertainment—a woman who simply writes?

Let me give you an inkling of what it's like here: I live without time—this state of atemporality soothes my husband. It's natural to Him. At first, I found it disorienting. Later, things got so bad that He took pity on me. We went on a long journey around the world, found ourselves among people. Real life rendered Him both reckless and vulnerable. He confided everything that I now plan to share with you. But then He had second thoughts; we packed and came back. Immediately after that, He disappeared. And here I am writing to you.

When I write to you, time exists once more. It shakes me, makes my skin crawl, because if time exists, then what am I doing here?

I FELL ASLEEP tied to that tree, but I woke up in bed. I was in the small windowless room from which I write to you today, next to the big bedroom that God and I now share. I did not know where I was or how I had got there, dry despite the deluge. The sheets smelled of detergent; their white borders rising and falling to the rhythm of my breath. I would have thought I was dreaming had it not been for the grooves my brother's ropes had gouged into my wrists.

An Angel sat next to me. The very first thing I noticed was its wings, whiter than a swan's belly. Never had I seen anything so exquisite. Its face was an ordinary face—unremarkable is the word that comes to mind. Closing my eyes, I immediately forgot its features. I gathered my wits about me, threw off the covers. The Angel rose too, leaving no trace on the sheets. I got out of bed and walked up and down the room, from wall to wall. It followed me. But still feeling weak, I went back to bed. The Angel also sat down at the very edge of the mattress. It spoke, an incomprehensible series of "*ffhhs*" and "*gggths*," peering at me as if expecting an answer. Its voice sounded like a tape recording, garbled and frayed from too much playback, buried deep in its belly. It pointed to a pitcher of water: "*Lklforihthothis? Kxhfhrieefsx?*" It made me drink.

I don't know how many hours passed like this. The room had neither window nor door, so I couldn't see when or if the sun had set. Eyes closed, I sniffed the plump pillow that brought to mind my aunt's washing, and from there, in natural progression, her hands smoothing fabric as she sat at the sewing machine. She used to hum as she sewed, a psalm or hymn, I don't know. She was a strange woman, but I missed her. The love I felt for her was the kind of love that is best grasped in a windowless room, in a prison cell. Everything I'd seen, everything I'd lived, reeled past my closed eyes like scenes from a movie: school; pranks at recess; my math teacher's wrist clasped by a weathered watch strap; the dimpled cheek of a boy I liked; my mother's hands rolling up the drawing paper; my father's feet on the low coffee table in the living room; the car spinning out of control (yes, I'll tell you about this soon).

There were freeze-frames, too: my aunt, my brother, motionless in the middle of an empty room; the streams of rainwater around the roots of the tree on the hill; the picture of my parents I kept in my pencil case. Random things: the electric light bulb in the kitchen that always used to buzz; the rug with the sky-blue rhombuses that lay in our hallway; the collection of paperclips I kept in the top drawer of my desk. I thought of them all as if they were and weren't my own, like relics of a bygone life, and everything I observed around me now—the bed, the Angel, the pitcher of water—were images of a new world.

Then, my lids fluttered half-open and there He was. My gaze travelled up the resplendent beard to meet His eyes, as pure and clear as a dog's. I took in the thick brows, the tousled hair. How to describe His body? It was as if He were trying not to frighten me. He was wearing arms and legs like others wear shirt and pants. He was sitting on the edge of the bed, where the Angel had sat earlier, wrapped in a robe, barefoot, toenails iridescent.

"Don't be scared," came a gentle, otherworldly voice.

I bowed my head. "I'm not scared."

"Here," He tipped my chin to make me look into His eyes. His pupils glistened, fiery and wet.

I now think that was a careless gesture, an unwitting encouragement of what Augustine called *superbia*, the sin of pride. Why would He force me to raise my head if He never intended to consider me an equal? Right then, the only thing I was sure of was that the air had thickened. His hand lacked substance, the tangibility of matter. He was holding my chin, but at the same time, my chin felt as if it was simply floating there, arrogant and jutting, independently of what I wanted it to do. And what exactly did I want? I don't know. I had never been so close to God.

Ever since I got hold of this pencil, I've been keeping notes. When I hear a sound, I hide it and open the Bible at a random page. My hearing has grown sharper: I discern the Angels swishing on the stairs; I know when they are about to knock on the door. Lately, I've taken to locking it. I don't know whether He told them about what happened on our journey. I don't know whether He communicates with them, or whether He too wants to be alone.

At night, I hide the pencil in the only place in the world where God will not think to look: my vagina. I bored a hole through the end of the pencil with a screwdriver; then I looped a string through it and tied three knots. At night, the string dangles between my legs, the pencil nestles wetly inside me. In the morning, I pull on the knots and the tip emerges from between my lips. I pull it out like I used to do with my bloody tampons. I no longer get my period, but I still know the feeling of something plugging my vagina.

It's almost time for dinner. I don't know whether He will deign to appear, but I will go down to the dining room like I do every night. I mustn't overdo it, shutting myself up in here with you. To avoid raising suspicion, it is vital that I stick to my regular routine; that I carefully hide my pencil, my paper, all the evidence. To my husband, evidence is an unseemly word, talk of miracles, unsavory. I made this discovery recently and after great effort. I don't want to upset Him, even though He deserves it. Love, however, eclipses my anger. Love and concern: Where is He? What is He doing? My mind always strays to something bad.

God does not believe in miracles, but I am asking you to. Put yourself in my position. From the beginning, I had two options: either to believe in miracles (what you and I would call a miracle) or to convince myself that I was making it all up: His hand on my chin, the Angel and the drink of water, the windowless room, the bed, the sheets.

Skepticism is something that comes later, much later, when, in conversation with others, you begin to make light of things, to pick them apart. He was my sole interlocutor. I shared His world, His views of the world. I fully accepted His generosity, His mystery; the fact that He didn't believe in miracles.

I beg you, don't go, no matter how strange the things I say. I ask that you believe in me, that you be patient until it all starts to make sense and the wider meaning becomes clear. Big, difficult questions demand complex answers. As for miracles, please bear with me when I say: for me the miracle is your existence, not His.

You find my wording odd? You ask how dare I speak of "unwitting encouragement" when I talk about God? Based even on the little I have told you, I insist that it is not hubris on my part to describe Him as unwitting. Given that He appears before me as an embodied being, how am I to regard Him as anything other than a person like you and me? With beard and toenails, with voice and spectral hand, He drew a stark line between the nature of divinity and what He wanted me to see. I can judge Him only by human standards, because they are the only ones He permitted me. Therefore, when I say that God acted unwittingly, I don't mean to offend your faith—whatever it might be—but rather my husband.

I REMEMBER HIS words, how He immediately went to the heart of the matter:

"I've been married many times. I'm faithful, bound by deep ties to my spouse, and farewells are always torture. Sometimes, I'm alone for two hundred, five hundred years at a time. But the day always comes when my solitude becomes unbearable, maddening. All I see before me are yawning abysses and deep, dark wells, even though the Angels assure me that nothing has changed. I'm looking for someone accommodating and mild-mannered like you. I need only one companion, not a multitude."

I nodded.

"I do not want to bother you or force my presence in any way," He added, with a smile. And then, more seriously, "I hope you understand that our relationship will be purely platonic."

I shrugged my assent.

"You may do whatever you want. Pick fruit in the Forest, wander around the rooms, read the books in the Library, or lock yourself up in here and cry. It happens sometimes. All this is yours; I want you to feel it's yours; to take it or leave it as you please, as you would with something of your own. The only thing I ask is that you curb your longing for reality, logic, analysis. You'll see that eventually time will disappear, along with space. One day, you'll wake up and have no further need for the world of things. Our union will then be complete."

"But . . ."

"I know, you have many questions: What is life like here? What is the experience of time? … But I can't have you making your decision based on my explanation of such things, for that would reduce what we are doing to a contract of sorts. In any case, it would take too long, don't you think?"

I bowed my head.

"You feel as if you have no choice? Here, look at me. It's the simplest thing in the world for me to send you back. You'll wake up and it will be as if you dreamed it all. You'll tell your aunt about the dream, you'll laugh about it together, and it will occur to her that it's been a while since she lit the icon lamp in honor of the saints. But, if it were up to me, I'd like you to stay and invite me fully into your heart."

"Like a nun?" I ventured.

"That's a human interpretation," He replied. "It implies guilt, despair. I have never asked for anything like that. The only thing I ask for is companionship and understanding. To share your life with me, if you want to."

He didn't say "our lives." He had chosen His words carefully, accurately, and I could not help but admire His directness, His serenity, the boundless power of His logic. He had talked about justice and freedom of choice, rather than feelings and passions. Yet strangely, He had touched my heart.

I accepted. I said yes, again and again. I was swept away by the melody of His voice, and, lurking behind it, the inevitability of my fate. His face beamed, white beard atremble. The room began vibrating around us, the walls turning silvery like seawater in the sun.

"So be it," He said.

I'M DIVIDING MY story into sections. First, what happened, then my reflections on what happened. We are not the same person at the beginning and the end of a story. We don't speak the same language or know the same things.

I've been preoccupied with what I started writing yesterday about the marriage proposal. I'm trying to describe what happened exactly as it happened, but the person I am now wants to speak out, to protest. Last night, after my solitary meal, as I stooped to blow out the candles, I looked at my husband's empty seat and thought: How can this be? Even if He chose me because I was accommodating and mild-mannered, as He put it, or devastated by a family tragedy as I would, why was I not wracked by doubt? Why did I not ask for some time to think about His proposal?

Shortly before I fell asleep, I pondered what and who I was when I first met Him. The image that came to mind filled me with sadness: long hair twisted into a braid, skin covered in freckles, lips forced into an awkward smile whenever someone addressed me. I was the kind of girl who never dares displease anyone, who thirsts for constraints, for trials and tribulations. A heart as shattered as mine beats furiously at the prospect of Absolute Love. In His proposal I saw an opportunity for ardor, for devotion. And what devotion! I was offered a life outside time and space that would finally put a stop to the clock ticking inside my head. The allure of devotion lies in its absolute surrender, its power to sunder us from our ties to the past.

At the same time, my need to believe was childish, shallow. I wanted to find someone, anyone, to whom I might boast about my accomplishment. Finally, God is at my side, I kept repeating to myself. God—God!—touched my chin! He talks to me! He showed Himself to me, not to bring back my parents or to take me to them, but—incredible as it may sound!—to marry me.

I imagined all the girls from my neighborhood and school, gawking in admiration and envy as I told them my story, embellishing it a bit, making Him younger and myself more eager. The girls were sure to ask about His eyes, and I would tell them something I hadn't thought about when He looked at me, for it had only occurred to me later, much later, when I was making every effort to render our first encounter worthy of the telling: "In His eyes, I saw the whole world, the clouds and the seas, the birds in the sky and the crops of the earth; I saw myself, my kindness and virtue, and everything vile and hateful had been wiped from the face of the earth." Today, if they were to ask me about His eyes, I would recite my favorite lines from the *Song of Songs*: "His eyes are as the eyes of doves by the rivers of water, washed with milk, and fitly set." Why hide it? My love for my husband was the kind of love that captivates at first, through its power and prestige, and later enslaves because of the impossible desire for something unattainable.

The girls would also be sure to ask about my studies, whether He was going to allow me to continue them. I wasn't stupid. I knew it was impossible. Setting off to university in the morning and then coming home in the evening to eat and sleep with the Creator of the world? Unheard of. Yet I wanted to go to medical school, like all the other brightest students of my generation. I yearned for a profession that would shield me from condescension and pity. I hungered for a creed that would buttress the very core of my being. I, who from a very young age had been so dependent on others, dreamed that one day they would depend on me: nurses, the sick, the families of the sick—all competing for my favor with reverence in their eyes.

In His presence, my dreams of saintliness were forgotten. No, to be more accurate, they were extinguished; uprooted in the irresistible rush of His will. I wonder: was it His idea to have my brother tie me to the tree? Did He send the storm? Was He testing me or simply observing my fate? But how is any of this important now? The coast is clear.

"God wants to marry you!"

His love is absolute, and absolute love does not come without trial and tribulation. If I wished to get married, He said, I had to open a door to the room and go outside. He didn't put it that way; He didn't want to frighten me. He simply said, "When you are ready, I'll be waiting for you in the Forest." Then, He disappeared, or rather He dissipated slowly, as if the lights had been dimmed.

Frantically, I scratched and scratched at the walls, tearing a fingernail as I did so. What was I to do? How could I open a door in the wall? I persevered, trying again and again, pounding the plaster, probing for springs and hidden passageways. On an impulse, I kept murmuring the prayer my aunt taught me: "O Lord of Spirits be with us, we have nobody to help us during our difficult times except You. Lord of Spirits, have mercy on us." Finally, I started beating my head against the wall. Tears rolled down my chin, my neck. The Angel behind me was all "*ffchhhh*" and "*Gthhh.*" *Ichdidtngsxx. Hrmnskftd.* I clutched onto its wings and begged. The Angel moaned "*krl*" without a trace of anger.

Worn out by my efforts, I fell asleep on the floor. I continued praying in my sleep. I don't know whether this was a dream or if I imagined it: On my knees in front of the wall, I mumbled incoherently, like my aunt at the sewing machine. At which point, an oak door, carved all over with birds and fruit, materialized. I opened my eyes and the door stood agape in the place where I had dreamed it. On approaching the landing, I was surrounded by motionless clouds. I remember thinking: He's teaching me how to pray. I cannot learn by myself, nor can anyone else teach me. He's teaching me how to dream purposefully, that I may achieve my goals. I didn't yet know about God's abhorrence for the word "purpose."

I closed my eyes and asked for a stairway. Instantly, it stretched before me. The treads became narrower and narrower; the twists and turns made me dizzy. I descended slowly, enveloped in thick fog. At the final turn, the air cleared. Before me lay acres of fruit trees, conifers, palms, a plethora of strange trees and flowers. In the distance, I could see a clearing; behind it, the dark columns of Forest. A semicircle of chairs surrounded a small stage. I had the whole of time to think, but I wasn't thinking. Never before had I seen so many yellow butterflies. They formed a cloud around me and I had to wave my hands in front of my face to shoo them away.

I needed clothes suitable for the occasion. I asked for them and they appeared: wedding dress, shawl, shoes; the dress's silk slip cool against my hands and belly. Taking my time, I turned towards the clearing. Monstrous birds perched on the chairs. As I drew nearer, I realized they weren't birds but Angels with folded wings. They were frightful to behold! From my vantage point, I could see where each wing tapered into a gnarled bone attached to the shoulder blade. This joint, so imperfect and grotesque, was covered in down. That was when the Angels lost some of their innocence and naturalness for me. But to this day, even now that I am fully aware of their role, I don't begrudge them anything. Without their intervention, the decision to go on our journey would never have been taken. Nor would I find myself here speaking to you.

He was waiting for me in front of the stage. Unlike in my drawing, He was holding not a bouquet, but two large candles. Dressed in a white suit, His eyes ablaze once more. What a mysterious being! I couldn't take my eyes from His face: resplendent, enchanting, full of confidence and something else, fearsome and unfathomable.

Offering me a candle, His hand touched mine without touching it, like before in the room. He helped me up the steps to the stage. To impress Him with my piety, I whispered the Prayer of the Hours, "Surround us with Your holy Angels, that guided and guarded by their host, we may arrive at the unity of the faith, and the understanding of Your ineffable glory."

He stared at me in surprise. "Ineffable glory?"

"That's what the prayer says. My aunt taught me it."

"Ineffable glory," He repeated, bemused. "Do you think so?"

And then, as if remembering that this wasn't the time for such talk, He added, "Okay, okay we'll have time for that."

"There's something else. May I ask one more thing?"

He turned to look at me.

"May my parents attend the wedding?"

"There are to be no witnesses at the wedding. It's an act of faith."

He didn't say they couldn't attend because they were dead, but rather because it was not done. I thought that maybe later He would allow me to see them.

"Are you ready?"

Heart beating, I imagined what it might be like to kiss God, to bury myself in His arms. For a second, I wondered whether He had a tongue, a chest, whether He knew how to sigh. The candle burned my fingers. Music came from the Forest, a babel of murmurs and chirps. The Angels said something in their incomprehensible language and God burst into laughter. I glanced up at Him inquiringly.

"I'll explain later," He said.

OUR MARRIAGE WAS neither religious nor civil. God does not believe in any of the things we think He believes in. "Marriage is an acceptance of the responsibility that comes with making a great promise," He declared at the end of the ceremony over which He presided. "If we call it a sacrifice, then marriage loses its meaning. It becomes a form of automatic reciprocity, shorn of vitality. You expect someone to save you, to teach you how to live." Everything He said was crystal clear. I didn't doubt it for a second. I liked the way He spoke, I liked the fact that all His wisdom was addressed to me.

Looking back on the ceremony now, I realize that the promise of eternal communion was mere words. God lives forever and remarries when His loneliness demands it. It is with silence that He greets my grievances, my concerns. To Him, each and every personal question is a betrayal.

We expect everything of God, and I more so than anyone. The more crises we experience in public, the more vulnerable we become. That is why there is a validity to the way strangers see us. It is from strangers that we learn shocking, life-changing truths about ourselves. Please don't think me blasphemous, but I dare say this also applies to God. It's as if whenever we curse, cry, or bid someone farewell, we are airing His failings. We constantly betray Him. Even though I'm afraid that my husband is betrayed mainly by Himself.

IN MY NARRATIVE, I have not yet found a way to distinguish between the creature I once was and what I am today. I fear that

the burden of what I know punctuates my narration and pre-
disposes you, my reader, to certain foregone conclusions while
draining me of my former vitality. Even though it seemed as if
I knew what I was doing back then, the fact was I didn't know
anything. And even though it may now seem as if I have lost my
mind, I know more than I ever did. I've been witness to untold
wonders, I've learned all there is to know about the creation of
the world. I know that at times Angels' wings fill me with joy and
at others, with terror. And that even God can be inconsolable.

I suppose you'll say: Perhaps what you see in His face is your
own inconsolability. Perhaps I see what I want to see; in other
words, a God who resembles me. You are both right and wrong.
He has changed, but that white sustenance—Despair—is as
essential to His nature as it ever was. He came from darkness—
it shapes everything He is.

I no longer remember the pure love I felt for Him, so it is
impossible to describe the past through the lens and the impact
of that love. I hope to approximate it for the sake of this story,
but I won't go so far as to depict dependence as a virtue. You see,
I no longer believe that a vulnerable heart is something worth
striving for. Religion trains people in the art of this dependency,
as does marriage. Oh, what on earth am I doing? Here I am,
holding forth, splitting hairs like a pedant boring the pants off
guests at a cocktail party or reception. I've never been to a reception, but I've read a lot about them in novels. Enough, at least, to
know that I will never have that kind of conversation with you.

As a matter of fact, the two of us will never speak. You will
have to make do with my monologue. And I, in my turn, will
try to anticipate your questions. Perhaps at this point you'll want
to ask: You no longer love Him? Is that why you're betraying
Him? I'm not betraying Him any more than He already betrays
Himself. I know about Him what He wants me to know. As for
love: I now love Him with an intensity greater than ever, to the
point of distraction. Yet I also hate Him with a passion: I want
to destroy Him.

What is at stake is whether I'll succeed in describing the love
I felt for Him at the beginning of our relationship. Chances are,

I'll fail. I don't remember what it is to love purely, to yearn to meet another's requirements, to drop all the playthings of your life and blot yourself out—gleefully, voluntarily—to make room for love. This kind of guileless love, of awestruck, fawning admiration is reminiscent of dogged religious devotion. A devotion intimately tied to our aspirations to transcendence—at least, that's what people say.

I don't know if I am making myself clear—am I? I'm talking of the idealized love we dream about when we place our hope in God without ever having met Him, about love as a trial by fire. We long for someone to reward us for the sufferings of our trials, and that someone is our Heavenly Father. We believe that salvation lies in directives sent to us from above, because that's the way we are constituted: we need directives for everything. But this too is a conversation for receptions, or a visit to a convent.

From a distance, fate looks very much like a choreographed dance: gestures obeying the dictates of randomly patterned chance. At school, our mathematics teacher told us about the problem of the higher powers. She used to say that if you roll the dice enough times, millions and millions of times, you will eventually obtain every possible combination of numbers.

After the ceremony, we sat in the front row to receive the Angels' presents and blessings. First, they knelt in front of Him, then they placed their unearthly limbs on my knee. In my arms, they laid the bouquets of flowers they had brought with their gifts. The flowers' scent reminded me of the sickly-sweet smell of the wreaths at my parents' funeral. Half buried under their bouquets, I begged them with my eyes: Take them off me! Please, take them off! Two Angels helped me pile the flowers on two nearby chairs.

I was watching the Angels carefully, trying to imprint their faces on my memory. The two Angels who had helped me were indistinguishable. So was the first Angel, the one I'd grabbed and shaken in the laundry room. Surrounded by an abundance of feathers, their features seemed instantly to dissipate, to melt away. They were expressionless and identical—a horde of celestial clones. At one point, God offered me His arm. I got up and we walked side by side, trailing a procession of Angels bearing gifts. In the distance was my new home. A white, domed four-storey building. I hadn't seen it when I descended the twisting staircase because I hadn't turned to look back.

How I longed to share the news with someone, anyone! I pretended that I was in the town square with my old classmates, talking about our latest infatuations. When it was my turn, my friends asked what was going on in my life. I shrugged nonchalantly and said: "I'm already married, but I can't tell you to whom. He's extremely famous and He likes His privacy." They rattled off the names of actors and soccer players. I pitied their provincialism.

Such vainglorious thoughts were unworthy of God's wife. I resolved to live up to my new responsibilities as soon as possible. I resolved to practice the type of grafting I'd seen on the Angels, but instead of wings and shoulder blades, I'd be grafting humble thoughts onto my prideful ones. Yes, I would sprout wings of a different kind.

My new husband was a gracious host. He showed me around my new home, leading me from room to room. He opened doors and stood back to let me pass. At one point, in my excitement, I exclaimed, "My God!" and He turned, thinking I was addressing Him. In every room, I ran my hands over the furniture, the curtains. He just stood there, and I didn't know whether my effusiveness pleased or wearied Him. I ought to be more spontaneous, I thought, and not worry about what He thinks of me.

The Heavenly House was all black and white. Armchairs, sofas, velvet pillows. Dark wooden tables, candles and candlesticks, net curtains. Everything was functional, symmetrical, simple. There were no mirrors to be seen, nothing purely decorative, or incongruous, or in the way. My husband asked my opinion about every little thing. He encouraged me to change whatever struck me as inappropriate or inconvenient. "No, no," I insisted. "This is the house of my dreams. When I lived in an apartment with my parents and later with my aunt, I always dreamed of a house with an interior staircase. Really. A house just like this."

The House has now lost its allure. It feels like an empty shell that bears witness to my failure, my joylessness. It screams of the struggle between body and spirit, familiarity and estrangement. Armchairs yell, "Why are you sitting?"; doors screech, "Hurry up, move it!" I have nowhere else to go. No other table to write on. No other bed on which to lie down and sleep.

I'm in a terribly bad mood. Today, even the air in this laundry room is like poison. At the outset of a plan everything seems easy; it's wreathed, so to speak, in the aura of divine grace. Now I must enter that small room without windows all alone. Blindly, I dig a well within myself, seeking words that I forgot existed; words that mean something. I extract them and examine them as if they were precious stones: Love, Faith, Freedom, Atonement. I find a word that warms my heart: Rebellion. I believe in it like I once believed in Him. I will keep my nose to the grindstone of my writing. Mine will be a practiced and carefully planned rebellion.

I haven't yet described the House to you. I must go on, because if I leave it, it will leave me. It's so easy to abandon myself—Oh, I am a master of self-abandonment! I lie in bed and focus on a spot on the ceiling. I stare at it and let myself sink, fathoms-deep, into God's timeless universe. Turbid water rises in the room, slowly, torturously, threatening to drown me.

On the ground floor are the kitchen, dining room, and rooms for the domestic help. On the second floor are the bedroom, laundry room, and bathroom (for me, since obviously God has no need of a toilet). On the third floor is the only room I may not enter, the Conference Room where my husband confers with the Angels. On the top floor is His Study, the domed room. During our honeymoon, it was closed. "We'll look inside another time," He said. "If we go in now, I'll get distracted and it will hold things up." He'll get distracted? By what? Why did He use that word? Is He trying to play down the distance between us? Ah, a tell-tale sign of His feelings for me, I thought. So perhaps He does think about me the way I think about Him. Is He mulling over which word I prefer, what kind of reaction? Does He smile like that at the Angels, or only at me? I tried imagining Him in His Study, sitting there scribbling our initials over and over, love-struck.

Immediately afterwards, in my mind's eye, as lifelike as can be, I saw His mouth twisted into a grimace: Ha, got you! Did you really think I needed a space like that, a room of My Own?

What if it were all staged? What if He had arranged the House that way out of compassion or, even worse, hypocrisy? What if the rooms were designed just for me? Spaces where I might lean back against a sofa, eat, pee. I immediately dismissed this thought. In order to live with Him I had to shake off the doubting Thomas within.

Why do my present anxieties insist on interrupting my story? Perhaps because my husband has disappeared without warning. As soon as I finish writing for the day, I climb up to the Study. I knock, but there's no answer. I open the door: no one. Only the dome and the books, His bergère, Wittgenstein's ladder, rose-tinted windows through which the day's dying rays quiver. Where could He be? Is He punishing me because I abandoned Him first? Or is this His way of proclaiming His power?

I never thought Him a hypocrite. I want you to know that my gratitude for the Heavenly House was immediate and genuine. I used to call it "our House," "my House." Rooms, pillows, frying pans reminded me of my mortality, of my need for clothing, food, caresses. Occasionally, I would be a bit more clearheaded about it: The House had obviously been built for the very first woman He fell for. The more He avoids the verb "fall," the more stubbornly I cling to it. "Tell me about Your wives," I insist. "How did You choose them? What was their skin like? Their eyes? Their voices? Which was the cleverest, which the nicest? How many have there been? Where are they buried?" When I pepper Him with such questions, He finds an excuse to leave the room. God's way of saying that the conversation is over.

We heaped the wedding gifts in the living room, where I was to open them at my leisure. The Angels had given me decorating books, classical music records, silk pajamas, air fresheners, a teapot, egg cups, a plush bathrobe. I had resolved to open one gift a day, but couldn't resist. Within three days I had opened them all.

Our ceremonial wedding candles stood in two metal brackets in the bedroom. On our wedding night, my husband switched on His bedside lamp. He leafed through a book on Renaissance art. I didn't know what to do, where to put my hands. I hadn't brought a book to bed, and it didn't seem right to turn my back to Him and go to sleep.

"What was it the Angels said during our wedding that made You laugh?"

He looked up from His book and smiled.

"Oh, nothing, just a joke: A man says, 'My wife and I were perfectly happy for thirty years. Then we met each other.'"

We laughed. Then He opened His book again and I glimpsed snatches of images: male thighs; cascades of women's hair carved in marble; lace; cloaks; soft round bellies; the male sex. When I fell asleep, I dreamed about our wedding. In my dream, my parents were there, at first as blank-eyed statues, but then they broke through their casts and emerged wearing clothes familiar to me from their wedding photograph. They watched the ceremony and, at the end, approached tentatively to congratulate us. "We are her parents," they announced. Puzzled, He responded, "But she's an orphan." Heads bowed, my parents re-entered their statues and let the marble swallow them up. I did not have time to say good bye.

EARLY DAYS AT the House: running up and down the stairs, roaming through the rooms, dancing in front of the curtains. After my parents' death, I stopped taking ballet lessons, but I remembered the *pas de chat*, the *pas de cheval*, the hyperbole of an *arabesque penché*. How wonderful it would be to dance with my husband, to do a *grand jeté* into His arms. How I would have loved to do with Him what other couples do when no one is looking! Occasionally, I abandoned myself to daydreams: God and I at a party, dancing in the middle of the dancefloor, surrounded by clapping couples. After a final, dramatic twirl, I lean against His shoulder, completely spent.

At the House, I didn't have to cook or clean; I had no responsibilities. There were no dinner parties or receptions. For whom? Neither saints nor family lived nearby, and as for the Angels, they had no stomachs. Besides me, no one needed to eat. That's why food became my primary pastime, a testament to my difference. I asked for soup and—poof!—it appeared in a bowl, creamy and rich. Strawberries bloomed in my palms. Fountains of water gurgled. After the miracle of the oak door, I had developed a knack for calling into being anything I desired. Even the weather bent to my whims. Rarely, flocks of clouds gathered, but I always succeeded in banishing them as long as I wished for it with all my heart.

In the kingdom of God, light is absolute. The House emanated an innate luminosity. There were no utility poles, computers, wires, sockets. The same thing outside the House. The brightest of lights—I'm at a loss to describe the quality of that brightness. Everything was so white I couldn't stop thinking about holiness. Suffice it to say that nothing broke, split, or wore out. In the Forest, leaves fell from trees into symmetrical piles. Garbage, shacks, dead branches, rotten fruit were nowhere to be seen. Nor were cracked pavements, weeds, imperfections. The water of the lake beyond the clearing never lost its clarity. The Angels never lost their temper.

On Sundays, I'd find them by the steel fence surrounding our living quarters. How did I know it was Sunday, you ask? I counted. What I can't fathom is how they knew what day it was. On Sundays, free of their duties, they congregated by the fence to play soccer. They played without keeping score, sprinting as fast as their narrow tunics allowed. Their wings stirring almost imperceptibly, a soft flutter like ghostly applause. The whole point of the game was to pass the ball. No-one ever scored. At first, I joined them, but I quickly tired of the lack of denouement and my visits became few and far between. During the week, early in the morning, the Angels would visit God in his Conference Room. In vain, I'd try to eavesdrop. I made out familiar sounds, "krlll" and so on. But I had no idea what was going on in there.

And what about Him? Oh, He was my comfort. I lived for the hour, a little before nightfall, when He appeared in the Forest. So as not to frighten me, He would make His way to me slowly, like a gradually expanding beam of light. He always approached from the House, a book tucked under His arm, waving as He neared. There was no sight more beautiful than His face, His long hair wafting in the breeze, the slight incline to His head that made it look like He was consenting, consenting to everything. I would stop what I was doing and listen to the cheery snapping of twigs under His feet. In gratitude I'd whisper under my breath the psalm my aunt had taught me: "Be merciful unto me, oh Lord, be merciful unto me, for my soul trusteth in thee: yea in the shadow of thy wings will I make my refuge. Oh, Lord, my heart is ready, my heart is ready." One after the other, the names of God that I used to jot down in my notebook, mainly the ones I hadn't understood at the time, echoed in my head: *Behold, the Lord of Hours; He Who delights in the Word; the Incorruptible; He Who is Outside the Firmament; the King of the Present; Behold Him who stretches out the heavens like a tent curtain.* And I would think to myself: Of course, I will take Him in my arms, come what may. This is what love means: to take whatever is given you, when it is given you. I learned to love Him the way one loves a snail curled up in its shell; I learned to make do with empty arms, with the celestial chest that hardly had the heft to hold me when I fell upon it.

There is amplitude and awe in walking beside your Beloved, in basking together in the shade under a plane tree. You behold the world He lays before you—no matter how illusory it might be—and it is as if you are witness to the pure gold of Creation's first prospect. At His side, you writhe with yearning for His words, for the infinite promise held by His silence. His laughter is never enough. When it withers and falls silent, your only desire is to grasp His hand and say the words that will make it bloom again.

God never opened the book under His arm. Instead, He placed it by His side on the grass, as if He had taken it out for a stroll. If He asked what I was thinking, I would say "You," and like a bashful boy, my husband would bow His head. Then, I would curl up in His arms, my cheek resting on His barely embodied knees until nightfall.

IN BED, I wracked my memory to come up with jokes and amusing anecdotes. He liked some more than others. Then He would laugh, and I would, too. Especially at jokes tailormade for me: "When you talk to God, you're praying. When God talks to you, you've got a screw loose."

He was enthused by a quip of Thomas Paine's—Benjamin Franklin's friend—which we had learned at school: "It would have approached nearer to the idea of a miracle, if Jonah had swallowed the whale." Oh, how my husband laughed! Every now and then, He'd remind me: "Tell me the one about Jonah again."

"I just remembered a good one about heaven," I said one day. He snapped His book shut and smiled at me encouragingly.

"Heaven, as conventionally conceived, is a place so inane, so dull, so useless, so miserable that nobody has ever ventured to describe a whole day in heaven, though plenty of people have described a day at the seaside."

"That's no joke," He snapped. "It is something that George Bernard Shaw once said."

"I'm sorry," I mumbled. "I didn't know. I didn't mean to make You angry."

"You didn't. It's playwrights and their smug cynicism that make me angry."

Abruptly, He turned off the light.

It was the first time I'd ever seen Him angry. And I, who modeled myself on His image and dreamed of one day becoming like Him, realized that the body and its feelings condemned me to a different fate. The little I retained from conversations with my aunt had led me to believe that divinity was within my grasp. To become one with God, one merely had to bridge the distance between.

But His anger filled me with doubt. You're the one who's to blame, I said to myself. You fall far short of the mark and cannot apprehend the truth of His being. You underestimate Him, deem Him capable of mediocrities. And He, for His part, reacts to the human passions that you project onto Him. You're the one who's doing it. Like a bird worshipping a winged Creator, or a tigress in awe of a hunting and disemboweling God.

If my thoughts were well-intentioned, I decided, my husband would be proud of me. So I started agonizing over everything

I said before I said it. I tried to forget the anthropomorphic God sitting beside me and instead to address the entirely divine being who had decided to appear before me in this paradoxical way. It was exhausting. Whenever I felt the urge to talk to Him with tenderness, like at the beginning of our relationship, I bit my tongue and admonished myself: What if later I have to take it all back? It is foolish to lay bare every stirring of my heart. I completely clammed up.

Then, I went to the other extreme: I got angry. I blurted whatever popped into my head. Doors started slamming shut behind Him. He was on the brink of telling me to go hell. The only reason He didn't was because He restrained Himself. Unlike me. When He had enough of my insistence, my nagging, He would scowl (or I imagined He did) and leave the room fuming and fulminating.

Let me explain: when I write that He fumed/fulminated and thundered/slammed the door behind Him, I am describing my reality. I stare at Him, expecting something from Him—be it reward, be it punishment. But God is inscrutable. If we were the parts of a casement window, I would be the handle, He the crank that supposedly sets everything in motion. But it is the hand that actually does the hard work of turning the handle and swinging the pane open.

Let me put it another way: this is how I see things. If you were to ask God and He were to reply in a language you understood, I don't know what He would say about us.

OFTEN, IN THE middle of the night, I open my eyes and, terror-stricken, I wonder: What if He ceased to exist? What if He were to die? What if those venomous philosophers were right when they declared Him dead and vanished from our world? The Angels surround me at the breakfast table and reassure me with their blunt, bird-like caws. But what if they are caws of agony? Now that I am aware of the Angels' secret, I no longer trust them: Do they know that I know? Are they endowed with intuition or only wings?

I eat alone. I sleep alone. And worst of all: I think alone. I would prefer to write to you after having spent some time reading, arguing with my husband. I would feel less sinful. But less free, too. I would address you differently if I knew that He was in his Study, reading while I wrote.

It's strange: as soon as I decided to do something of my own, He vanished. A terrible coincidence, like the ones you come across in novels.

I DECIDED TO put my new powers to the test: I would walk over the waters of the lake, fly over the Forest. My first attempt happened while I was sitting on a swing the Angels had built for me from a wooden plank and two thick ropes. There I was, swinging higher and higher, when suddenly I decided to let go and see what would happen. Kicking my legs like a swimmer, I rose into the air. Butterflies swarmed around me—not belligerent, merely numerous. I swatted at them to clear my way. Occasionally, during an abrupt mid-flight twist or turn, I hurt my foot or scratched my calf on a branch. Such small accidents did nothing to deter me. I loved the thrill of flight, the hurtling head-on rush, the frantic flailing of arms and legs during ascent. I remember such a surge of stimuli, such a wild succession of colors, I barely had time to form a thought and hold it clearly in mind before it sparked another. This mental hyperactivity had me raring to go, ready for anything at any time. I'd plunge head-first into the lake, dive deep, and then struggle my way back to the surface again. Clothes heavy with water, my only concern was to go faster and faster, wind lashing my face, drying my hair. The euphoria of flight, the shrieks of freedom, my burning blood, the vibrancy and pulse of motion—they all had me asking: Is my husband right? Am I shedding my body? Am I turning into air?

But no. No matter how far I flew, I could see no variation in the sequence of trees; in their spacing, their density. I would return to the House in a strange mood. Flight primed me for an elevation of the soul that was impossible to achieve under the circumstances. Elevation implies a distancing from terror, from degradation. But I had no truck with wars, crimes, shipwrecks, betrayals, airplane crashes. Worse still, I no longer cared. With the passage of time, my interest in what we call real life kept waning.

One evening, on our return to the House from the Forest, I looked up at the sky and noticed there was no moon. I thought that perhaps it was a new moon and waited for it to come out—but no, nothing. What about the light then? Where did the light come from? How did it shine and fade like that every day? Had He done it so that I would not begin to doubt? Not only was there no dust, not only did no flower wilt in the vase, but also the sun, the moon, the entire universe were missing. Life as I knew it had been replaced by an immaculate cardboard cut-out. Without east or west, I lost all sense of direction and along with it, the delusion of being able to do anything I wished. I became terribly depressed. And so, the changes began.

I stopped walking on water, flying over the trees of our Forest. No longer did such activities interest or amuse me. Sometimes, out of sheer boredom, I decided to cook. Tears streamed from my eyes as I peeled an onion. Or I pricked my fingers with pins while darning a sock. Angels bearing tissues appeared out of nowhere. I suspected that, like the furnishings, they came with the House. I did not understand them, nor could I bring myself to love them. Their kindness—how can I put it? It smacked of premeditation, obligation. What was I supposed to do with a love that presented itself as the only solution? But I am getting ahead of myself. I am starting to build walls without even digging the foundation: my own definition of love.

INFATUATION TURNED TO love when my husband started reading His books to me as I lay beside Him in the Forest, serene and carefree, watching the flutter of butterfly wings. Leaning against the trunk of our chosen tree, a plane with thick roots, I finally stopped trying too hard. I finally stopped worrying about what He thought of me. The plane tree basked in our love. We were a couple—a true couple.

His books did not interest me. When they chanced to fall open at a random page, I never understood a word, despite the fact that they were the work of human authors, mainly philosophers and theologians. The truth is, I did not really want to understand; abstract ideas bored me. Mathematics, problem-solving, I found mildly entertaining, but my greatest joy in those years was the complete avoidance of thinking. After everything that had happened, I was tired of thinking, despairing, fearing. I had not counted on God, who, at the very same time, decided to educate me. I don't know whether it was because my passivity perturbed Him, or whether He longed for greater intellectual stimulation. All I know is that He started with simple little questions about my childhood years, about my family. What they brought to mind was not pleasant, but the fact that I could put it all in order and tell my story comforted me. Ever since those early days, when I used to crumple up and discard my drawings, order has been for me the greatest of virtues.

But there's something else, too. I don't remember who said it: God enters through our wounds. During those rare hours in the clearing, He entered me in a way that no man ever enters a woman. Perfectly, purely, inscrutably. We talked. And our words radiated meaning. Without the Word there is no moral sensibility. Do you agree? And the point, the meaning of our lives, is revealed in the stories we tell. With all my heart, I hope you agree. And that—in a wrinkle of space and time as yet unknown to us—you are reading everything I have written to you.

THE TIME HAS now come for the Joker of Despair.

It was a Sunday, a few years after the drawing-of-God episode. Our parents announced a family drive to the beach. We rarely went on such outings. Father worked as a ship's cook and was always at sea. At home, he had no idea how to interact with my mother or us, his children. He did not know what to do with his hands. Occasionally, he would make fruit compote for us, the way they made it on the ships. He would ask how we were doing at school only then to stare at us absently, as if at waves rippling across the water.

Father was a restless soul, always chasing after an elusive something or other. I believe he chose that job of his in order to give everyone, and above all himself, the slip. He was like a visitor in his own home. Wearing only his shorts, he would watch sports on the television, his thick, sunburned calves resting on the low coffee table in the living room—something strictly forbidden to the rest of us. It would be in stormy seas that he turned to God; that was when everyone on the ship prayed. Or in mild weather, with the water glimmering on the far horizon. "You turn to God in joy or devastation," he used to say. "The rest of the time you don't give a damn."

Mother did not believe in God; she believed in order. Our sweaters were folded so meticulously, they did not to look like sweaters. When serving our meals, she poured exactly the same small puddle of sauce on each plate. Meat appeared on its platter in perfectly even slices, as if measured with a ruler. Whenever we entered a church, she would quickly duck her head before the icon of the Virgin and peck the glass before wiping it with the edge of her sleeve to erase any smudges. Anyone who didn't know her might have mistaken her to be devout. She often repeated phrases like: "God help us!" and, "God forbid!" and, "By the grace of God."

That Sunday, the grace of God was not with us. I remember the pallid light outside the kitchen balcony. Forehead pressed to the window pane, I whined: I didn't see why we all had to go to the beach when father had had more than his fair share of the sea. Mother declared that it was her idea; she was going stir-crazy indoors and had a hankering to go, my whining be damned. She fried some meatballs, packed tomatoes and apples in the Tupperware, tossed some bananas in a plastic bag. She asked me to wrap the hardboiled eggs in aluminum foil, each separately. When everything was ready, mother kicked off her shoes and gave her feet a good rub. "Aaaahhhhh," she sighed, "I needed that."

That sentence has stuck with me because very shortly afterwards, she no longer needed anything. We were on the main road, our car wheezing around a blind bend. My father had his hand out the window, to point at the sea, and mother was biting into an apple, when the truck lurched at us. Screeching brakes. Exploding glass. When I opened my eyes, the windscreen was shattered. My parents' unnaturally contorted bodies lay on the tarmac.

Festooned with Mother's bite marks, the apple spun on the

mat at my feet. At the hospital, I slept clutching the rotting apple until a nurse wrested it away from me. When we recovered, we were taken to Auntie's house. Every night, I waited for my parents to turn off the light. I could still hear their voices: "Are you still awake?" and, "Have you brushed your teeth?" In time, their voices started to fade, like the songs we sing out of tune because they're no longer played on the radio. I didn't want to cry. But when my aunt switched off the light, I was wracked by sobs underneath the sheets. Mainly for mother, but also a little for father.

In one of the pockets of my pencil case, next to the colored pencils, I hid my parents' wedding photograph. It was the only one I could find of the two of them together. There were pictures of Father aboard ship, and others of Mother from the time before she met him (usually two or three girls leaning against a fence or the hood of a car, surrounded by daisies). In the wedding picture, their heads were touching. He was wearing a suit with a bowtie, she a long satin dress. They looked beautiful, ethereal, like saints. In class, when I finished my exercises, I would secretly take out the picture and pray.

I looked mainly at mother because she was beautiful and more familiar to me. I liked everything about her: her green eyes, her delicate wrists, her lips, parted as if she were about to speak. When nobody was looking, I would press my ear against those lips in case she thought of something to say to me. At home, I would tune in to one of the golden-oldie stations and dance with the photograph. Mother adored music and dancing. Even when she was doing chores, she was in the habit of turning on the radio and swaying to the music. When I clapped, she would laugh, flush, and glance at the floor as if she had done something naughty. I wondered whether mother begrudged her imprisonment at home; whether she longed to be dancing freely, up on her toes, surrounded by admiring eyes. Even trapped in that picture, it was clear she was dying for a dance. Her smile was rapt, her lips parted, as the two of us twirled around Auntie's living room.

Auntie was father's sister. She, too, would cry in bed at night. I would hear her sniffling when I got up to go to the toilet. She had no children, no husband, no dreams. One of those women of yore, who sat by as time slipped away, washing over them as if they were stones. Her great love was her brother; when he went away to sea, she learned how to live alone. Now, she had us— our own little family. We went to school, did our chores, wept at night. Only the women, not my brother. My brother and I were never alike. He was coarse and callous. My parents doted on him, spoiled him rotten. After they died, he acquired new hobbies: torturing animals, smoking, petty theft.

God kept Auntie and me very busy. She explained the various ways He was referred to in the Holy Scripture. Religiously, I jotted those names down in a notebook: *God, the Preserver of All; the Unchanging; the Source of Light; He Who is Slow to Anger; He Who Forbears; He who is untouched in His seat; the Sweet Lord; God, Dominion of Dominions; the Rock of Scripture; He who weighs the mountains in the scales.* As I created long lists of God's epithets, tall mountains rose to encircle me in their embrace.

When Easter neared, Auntie would take me to hear the Twelve Gospels. I did not understand the words. She bent over to whisper Christ's appeal to His Father while nailed to the cross: "My God, my God, why hast thou forsaken me?" "Why?" I echoed. "He was not forsaken," Auntie replied. "Do parents forsake their children? Wait and you will see." But because I wouldn't stop asking and kept tugging at her skirt, Auntie took me out into the churchyard and explained that Christ was resurrected to live eternally at His Father's side. Her face inches from mine, her tears, the way she clutched my fingers as she spoke—I believed it all.

When we went back inside the church, God blessed us from the dome on high. With fluttering shadow and flaring candlelight, I painted mother's teeth and father's brow on His face. Under the clouds concealing His body, I imagined a trunk with four legs: two hairy, muscular legs, like father's; the other two warm and slender, like mother's. If I were crucified, might I finally be reunited with them? I closed my eyes and prayed with all my heart. "Almighty Father, crucify me, save me!" Nothing. The flicker of candle flames. The husky drone of cantors. The Saints, silent and still in their icons.

I turned to the person closest to me: my brother. I begged him to torture me, often and without fail. He demonstrated great ingenuity. At times, he obliged me to swallow grasshoppers; at other times, to lie motionless for hours in the chest beneath the couch, pretending to be Lazarus awaiting the Resurrection. As I lay there, I whispered: "Crucify me! Save me!"

Over Auntie's bed hung an icon of Christ crowned with thorns, eyes upraised to the ceiling. One day, as I prayed, I noticed a scratch in the paint that made Christ look as if he had a squint in one eye. I wanted to see if I could make the other eye squint too. Just like I used to pick at our Formica table, I started picking. When I was done, Christ was a pitiful sight: empty eye sockets, scratches around his neck, holes in his beautiful tunic. That night, Auntie roused me from my sleep. "What have you done?" "Me? Nothing!" She then accused my brother. "I don't give a damn about your stinking icons!" he screamed. Auntie believed us—she always did. She fell to her knees and crossed herself over and over again. I sat beside her and watched. How I pitied her! I did not stop going to church with her. I did not stop bowing to kiss the glass-sheathed icons. I still loved the Virgin, the dragon-slaying Saints. But the thought that God, that all the Saints, could turn monstrous overnight made my skin crawl.

As I grew older, I dreamed of meeting a boy. A good boy. A nice boy, who would take me far away. I imagined him: a torrent of light, piercing the beams of the ceiling and gushing in. I had a candidate in mind, a very quiet classmate of mine from middle school. One day, we were walking back home together from school, that boy and I. Night had fallen, and I talked, now tenderly, now dirty, in the hope that he would finally do something. The boy leaned over me, his whistling breath hot and heavy on my neck. Without warning, he grabbed my breast and gave my nipple a violent, prolonged twist. I burst into laughter and couldn't stop.

All the while, my brother kept inventing new ways to torture me. Months, then years pass, before we finally get to the day when he tied me to the tree.

GOD LISTENED TO my stories without comment. He let me speak until I'd had enough and either stopped or wept (I seldom wept). Only then would He ask a couple of questions. It wasn't clear to me what He was trying to get at with His questions. They were neither philosophical nor metaphysical, unlike those He asked later, when I started reading the books in the library. He wanted to know about my parents. About my brother. Whether I would have preferred to be an only child. He asked whether I was fond of my aunt. Whether I enjoyed school. Whether my friends stood by me, or whether I thought they had let me down. Difficult questions. It turns out that the answers to important questions are different each time. Depending on the context, anything might be true. I had friends; I didn't have friends. My brother tormented me; my brother adored me. Life without parents was a curse; life without parents was a blessing. Had they still been alive, I would not have felt the true weight of their absence.

Occasionally, my husband would hold forth. When I first told Him about mother's apple—about my attempt to save her bite marks—He expounded on the meaning of entropy, a system's gradual decline into disorder. An apple, He declared, is composed of a certain arrangement of particles in space. When the apple rots, those particles become disordered and entropy sets in. It is therefore futile to expect the regeneration of an apple from its remains. The moment was a somber one. God had acknowledged our ultimately homogenous distribution, the total entropy of the universe. He therefore shattered my one remaining illusion: a reunion with my parents in a place of tender grass.

Sometimes, He asked whether I had ever tried snails or ox tongue. Whether I had ever broken a bone. I eagerly answered such random questions. I believed in Him, and our conversations were always a revelation. Even when we began with something completely commonplace, I would end up talking about fear, disgust, despair, heartbreak. The thought of our parting filled me with terror, as did the silence at the end of His questions. It did not even occur to me to ask Him anything. I revered and respected Him. I believed that to ask Him a question would be to interrogate Him.

When I reached the age of twenty-one, I started asking questions. At the time, I still kept a tally of the years and knew my
age. For reasons I still do not understand, I was determined to
preserve an awareness of time. It was difficult. The simplest of
things in the human world are impossible in the kingdom of
God.

On my birthday, I wanted to parade before Him, one after
the other, the many questions troubling my heart. Why are we
brought into the world? What is this place? Where is it? Why
did You choose me? What happened to Your previous wives?
Have You had much interaction with other people? Where are
my parents? How did You make the world? And why did You
choose to make it like this and not some other way? Did You
feel lonely before? Were You always alone? Did You have a fully
worked-out plan for Creation or were You guided by instinct?
Were Your initial ambitions different than what came to pass?
Are You accountable to anyone or anything? Is there a devil? Are
there other gods? What does omnipotence mean to You? Do You
possess it, and if so, how? Why aren't there any newspapers in the
house? Shouldn't there be? Do You have a code of ethics? How
much do You intervene in human affairs, if at all? What is Your
opinion of the prophets of the various religious? To what species
do the Angels belong? What language do they speak?

But my only question was: "Do you know how long I will
live?"

He glared at me, eyes icy. We were sitting across from each
other, a fat slice of cake on our plates. It was my birthday, and I
had not expected a look like that. Whenever I insisted on something or became argumentative, He would get up and leave. This
time, He did not budge from His seat. He continued to stare at
me, terrible eyes aflame, beard turned to stone.

I looked down at my plate. "Am I being disrespectful?"

"You're being immature. Very immature. I am neither a
diviner nor a magician. Do you understand?"

I nodded. "I understand that You do not wish to be confused
with conjurers or magicians. And that it is wrong to misconstrue
the meaning of Your acts."

"Wrong and right are human concerns linked to your obsession with advantageous solutions and constant progress."

"Yes, but I'm not talking about myself, I'm talking about You. Does the fact that You do not believe in miracles mean that not everything is possible, even for You? Or are you merely punishing Yourself for the fact that You are, indeed, omnipotent?"

His eyes narrowed. "At the moment of Revelation our very being is revealed. You, however, have revealed yourself now. Your distress is . . ."

I finished His sentence: "Merely human."

That night, everything changed.

WHEN YOU ARE married to God, it is absurd to worry. He's not going to crash His car, be murdered, or fall victim to fraud unless He wills it. This does not reassure me. What worries me even more is the thought that whatever befalls Him is only what He desires, and that regardless, my lot is to brood and doubt. Oh, where is He hiding? Where is He hiding already? Why won't He give any sign of life? Is He angry at me or is He angry at Himself for believing in me? In the morning I'm content to have heaps of time to write to you, but as soon as night falls, I find the solitude crushing. Angels knock at the door and I turn to stone. I say, "Thank you, I don't need anything." I want to write to you without distraction.

At times, engrossed in thought, chewing on my pencil, I am transported back to the days of my childhood, to before my parents' death. I find it inconceivable that I was once a child, that I found such joy in my mother's company, that my brother and I quarreled in silence so that our parents would not hear. But mostly it is inconceivable to me that I was once a child who believed that my natural condition, my fate, was to suffer. There is mother, roaming the house in her sky-blue quilted dressing gown, vacuuming. My brother lies on the bed with his shoes on, eating corn puffs. Travel bag in tow, father comes and goes. I climb the trees on the ring road that I described to you earlier. Curled up on high branches like a cat, I weave necklaces and bracelets from pine sprigs. From on high, I spy on the city, its apartment blocks and cars. My town. My neighborhood. My street. All mine.

It is dispiriting to compare God's kingdom to the landscapes of my youth. Despite the smallness of the town I was from, it seemed big, dazzling, created especially for me: a miniscule blade of grass poking through a crack in a rock; mountain peaks outlined against the horizon; ancient temples, churches, squares; even the people strolling along or overtaking me in a hurry. When scenes like these appear before me, a pang goes through my heart. I need the horizon, I long for it with a passion. As if it were my father, or my surly brother.

Before, I used to fly searching for something to remind me of my homeland: olive groves, mountains, my beloved sea. No matter how far I flew, all I saw were lakes and identical paths through the Forest. Not a single hill, no matter how low, not the slightest variation in the view. I was not yet aware of my husband's distaste for mountains. And so, I couldn't help wondering: has He forgotten that He created the world?

GOD OBJECTED NOT to the quantity, but to the quality—the very nature—of my questions. To the fact that I had broken my vow of unconditional faith. Whenever I reminisced about my life before Him, He hunched up and listened, all ears. I would even go so far as to say that He empathized with me. And He asked questions, discreetly, in a low voice, as if not really asking, as if filling in the blanks. But when you ply someone with questions, you're asking for trouble, aren't you? Questions inevitably come back at you. So, yes, I started asking, and in order to escape, He sought refuge in evasion. "What do you mean by that?" "I don't know." "Perhaps."

Morning and evening without fail He joined me at the dining table. Even though He did not drink, we always clinked glasses. God has no stomach, no heart, no desires. No, there was never anything erotic between us. And children, of course, were out of the question. Ironic, right? He who created everything, cannot recreate Himself. This inability has engendered all manner of legends and doctrines, including the story of the Virgin Birth. God finds it amusing.

"It makes no sense whatsoever," He remarks. "But it is a nice little tale about overcoming desire."

"Nice for you, for Your legacy perhaps, but not for the Virgin. Did anyone bother to ask her consent before making a mockery of her love life like that?"

My husband bursts out laughing. "If only there were a Virgin; if only she had been the butt of a joke, as you put it. I wouldn't be so alone if that were the case."

Solitude: His weapon when the conversation strays into difficult waters. When He brings it up, an icy wind whistles through the House, through the Forest. Invariably, one of the Angels hastens to bring me the cardigan I knitted for such occasions.

GOD'S DESPAIR: His lack of forebears, a personal history, the sustaining warmth of family. That, at least, is what I believe. You think I'm inventing things? Why, then, did He keep asking for stories about my family life? I would describe the silliest things: how I used to fold the paper napkins when I set the table; how father slurped his soup; how my brother fiddled with his fork; how mother fluffed up the sofa pillows in the living room, even though it was only a matter of time before someone sat down and squashed them again; how, on Saturday evenings, we all squeezed onto the burgundy velvet couch and watched movies on the television.

God was mad about details. Who sat next to whom? Were we allowed to eat in the living room? Why did an argument always break out on those Saturday evenings? Did we ever move the furniture around? Did we go on family vacations? Who took out the garbage? How did we celebrate our birthdays? What presents did we children get? Did I like my presents, or would I have preferred different ones?

When my stories came to an end, He seemed breathless, human. The arms He wore for our meetings hung from His shoulders more naturally. Occasionally, He took my hand in His and we would just sit there, in silence. Sometimes, His words tore at my heart:

"You remember so many things. I have never heard another human being speak with such attention to detail."

"What's special about that?" I would ask.

"It's simple. I like your descriptions. They're so precise."

Perhaps it was something He said to all His wives. But I like to believe I was different. And I think I'm right—He would not have attempted a journey with me otherwise. Have I given you the wrong impression of our relationship? We humans tend to dwell more on the disappointments than the moments of joy. So, let me say it again: I loved Him and I love Him. Despair does not diminish love. God taught me how to love without hope, without fear. Like all couples, in moments of great happiness we discussed love.

I would ask: "Do You love me?"

But when He answered me, He would resort to catechism: "Remember Spinoza's words? The intellectual love for God is part and parcel of the infinite love with which God loves Himself."

"But I want to know what God has to say about that," I would insist.

"He agrees. He says that nothing exists outside God."

"I'm not nothing! And I don't care what Spinoza says. What do You say?"

"I do not say anything." God would reply. "I love."

Whereupon I would burst into laughter. Only later, in the darkness of our room, was I gripped with fear. What if God stopped loving? What would happen to love?

One day, I was telling Him about my childhood drawings. About how, in the middle of a white sheet of paper, I had sketched Him holding a bouquet of flowers. "As if I were human," He remarked. I then explained how, as a child, I was certain that He knew everything about me, that He had seen my drawing. My husband merely listened, inscrutable and impassive. He neither agreed nor disagreed.

The next day, as I was drinking my tea in the dining room, I looked up and spotted first a bouquet, then His hands wrapped around it. Jasmine, an unfamiliar variety.

"What do you think? Do I look like your drawing?"

I ran to fetch a vase for the flowers. Then, I threw my arms around Him—as always, scooping air.

These instances are frozen in time for me: testimonials of

tenderness, words heavy with meaning, moments when God, just like a hesitant lover, tore aside the veil of silence, ruefully to reveal the word "love." At such times, He always looked at me with eyes clamoring with His desire to stop talking; signaling how my insistence on questioning His love only destroyed His dream of it.

My dream is a selfish one. I am human and the body is the greatest sense of space I know. So, yes, I dream about His embodiment. Such a development would make me happy, the happiest woman on earth. Did I say "on earth"? But we are not on earth! I do not even know what it is we are on, above, or inside. There is no explaining this place where we live—it certainly does not explain itself. The Beasts in the Forest do not kill or disembowel. There is no currency of exchange. Neighbors, nations, secret treaties, oil pipelines, arms dealers, drugs, debt: all are absent. Nothing but an icy silence and the stillness of lake waters unblemished by the reflection of any moon.

WE DID NOT kiss at our wedding. My husband says that such things are mortal comforts. When He finds me curled up on the couch, He asks, "Why are you rubbing your shoulders? What is the point?" I turn then to Him and brush the anemic, tiny hairs on my arms with my fingertips. "See the blue bulge of veins?" I ask, stretching my arm toward Him.

"You place too much importance on the body."

I shrug. "It is what I know."

God does not understand. Displays of human nature are incomprehensible to Him, even though He, of all people, ought to know. Why, in creating the body, did He secrete within it such hunger for another's touch? Why did He make our bed, why did He lead me to it, if all He planned to do was turn on His side and fall asleep every night? Why in God's name does God sleep?

I did not want to offend Him. I did not want to demand of Him something He could not give. At night, as He slept, I discovered my body under the sheets. I began by fondling my breasts. Then, hesitantly at first but with increasing greed, burying one or two fingers in my vagina. Above the lips, there was a nub that I liked to knead as if it were a piece of dough. And another inside that hardened and gradually filled with tiny knots. Eyes shut, enrapt, I rubbed and stroked, resorting to a couple of tried-and-tested tricks to make myself come. They always worked: rapid, rhythmic spasms unwound coil-like through me, provoking stifled laughter. You, who know all about this, must find my ignorance laughable. But the truth is, I did not know. It was at such moments that I became aware of my existence. Yes, I was alive. An enormous heart pulsed between my legs.

I did not talk to Him about it. And I hope He never became fully aware of what was going on back then. Since then, I have managed just fine. Sex no longer concerns me.

IN THOSE EARLY days, I used to dream about God naked. Touching myself, I imagined His ghostly arms, "rods of gold," around me, His lips "a scarlet ribbon"—in the words of my favorite poem. I also fantasized about the Angels, what would happen if they were to lift their tunics and come at me, the entire flock of them at once. Sometimes I remembered the boy who tweaked my nipple, or the repulsive men from my childhood, like the fellow from the corner store who would come up from behind and grind against me when I went in there to buy chewing gum. "Where is my love?" I whispered into my pillow and—poof!— it took the shape of a man. Later, when I gained a little confidence, I started going to the Forest. Oh, how to tell you this? Is there any point in sugarcoating it? No, I will describe everything exactly as it happened.

It started accidentally: the body, the victory of dreams, or perhaps its defeat. One night, there I was, grinding against a tree-trunk, trying to accomplish what I usually accomplished alone in bed while my husband slept. I liked the dark. Under its soft gusts of wind, I saw my body expanding into the immensity of sky. Invisible life enveloped me: rustling leaves, bestial growls and grunts, the sudden slither of a snake beside me. It didn't scare me. At first, I thought it looked like the Rainbow Serpents of the Aborigines, sentries to quartz crystals in the mystical texts I had started reading in the Library. And my snake did look like a sentry, grim and deadly. It turned out to be sensual and persistent instead. Scales shimmering in the dark; forked tongue exploring me in places no one had ever explored.

The Forest became a second home to me after that. Every night, I romped, no, I wallowed, with the Beasts: hyenas, lions, tigers. (Unfortunately, the snake never appeared again). Sprawled at the foot of a tree, perched on the lip of a rock. splayed long and empty and always as far as possible from the clearing, I waited with my dress lifted high over my waist. The Beasts sniffed me out. Emerging from their lairs, they rose to the occasion. Their snouts snuffling between my thighs, they penetrated everything they could. Eyes fixed on a point in the distance, on the sky or spiky tree branches, I feigned indifference at first. Perhaps I wasn't really feigning. I suffered the Beasts' every thrust as if the only reason for my being there was to endure their assaults. But was there any resistance on my part? No, to ease their thrusting, I pulled my underwear to the side, so that it dug deep into my flesh.

I do not mean to offend or shock with this account. What happened in the Forest, however, was without precedent. The way to make sense of it is not to imagine two or more random bodies in the throes of lovemaking (note that the Beasts would often arrive in twos or threes, grunting as they waited their turn). Those abhorrent interludes of mine found no place in any existing sexual scenario. There were no caresses, no foreplay, no ebbs and flows of desire. There were no words: "I want it," "I can't stand it," "slow down," "turn over," "again." We came from different worlds; worlds to which we inevitably returned after our copulation. I cannot invoke the exchange, the complementarity of roles one finds in nature. The Beasts did all the work. I cannot speak of constraints or hesitations. I imposed no rules on that disgusting game. Like a mouse in the paws of a cat, they turned me this way and that as they pleased. And as soon as they found a position to their liking, they gripped me, talons and teeth sunk deep in my buttocks, my neck, my belly. Using my fingers, I'd clear the way and pull their organs towards me, fearful that in their haste to find a warm, welcoming orifice, they would gouge one in my flesh.

You are probably wondering: If the sex was as degrading as you say, why did you keep going? Because gradually I succumbed to it. That is the truth. In the company of the Beasts, I too learned to let myself go, to release my inner beast. And once the final vestiges of resistance had been overcome, my hidden self crawled out, fawning and obscene. The frenzied Beasts rode me, pinned me down, and I writhed beneath them, circling around and around a cesspool, lewd groans and growls the likes of which I have heard neither before nor since spewing from my mouth. Therefore, I too must have been getting something out of that torment. Don't ask me what. All I can say is that I willingly yielded to their furious assaults, and when I could take no more, I would rest my cheek or elbow on the earth to prop myself up. Even then, like a thrown wrestler who refuses to concede the bout, I would turn to stare my Beast in the eyes. The entreaty in mine never failed to further inflame the Beast, to heighten the frenzy of its grappling and pounding. Growling, it would plunge in and out of me. Brutally. Savagely. As if trying to annihilate me. When finally it fled, I lay half-conscious in the dust. A broken seal, a scarlet stain upon the earth. Biting my hands so as not to scream. Yes, it was a sick craving, but I couldn't do without it.

Trembling, almost swooning, I'd make my way back to the House. Don't forget that each time, I was unprepared for what the Beasts would do to me; each time it was different. Stunned, bloodied, legs scratched and body covered in bruises, I locked myself in the bathroom to scrub my flesh. I always tried to change the sheets. I longed to lie on clean, freshly-ironed bedclothes.

If my husband happened to be in bed, I would tiptoe to Him and kneel at His side. I liked to watch Him in the dark. How I loved Him, how I pitied Him at such moments! Eventually, my eyelids drooped and I too crept under the sheets. I nestled up to Him, careful not to wake Him. I groped His hazy outline, my hands sinking between His invisible loins. Was I imagining things or did His body loosen its grip on corporeality at night? Then again, what if He did it on purpose, to punish me? Or to prove to me (airhead that I was) not only that He had an inner life, but that He *was* interior life, a primordial form of understanding, an inconceivable idea? He started going to bed earlier and earlier, lying at the very edge of the mattress, leaving a vast emptiness between us. I did not know what to do with all that empty space. In despair, I clung to Him.

DID HE KNOW? I believe so. I also believe that, deeming my experiments part and parcel of human nature, He resolved not to intervene. He did not want to keep an eye on me or make me feel like He was keeping an eye on me. Instead, here and there, discreetly, strategically, He would plant some Augustine or Plotinus; texts by the Stoic philosophers on the serenity of the inner life; Orphic dicta lauding sexual abstinence and restraint of the Dionysian passions; Plato's musings on the lower beings that dwell in the depths of the earth and their brutalizing influence on the body; and some Emerson as well: his musings on virtue and necessity.

Eager for meaning and direction, I read through the lens of my own obscenities. I read the way He wanted me to read: as if holding in my hands the encrypted map to a great treasure. Even though I did not understand much, I was enthralled by philosophy, which instantly soothed my itch to play with the Beasts. At Plotinus's urging, I sought the pearl of the soul that languished beneath the shell of skin. Nevertheless, in the end I always surrendered, again and again, to the bodily urge.

My husband was omnipotent; He occupied my mind. At the mere thought that He knew, that He suspected, the pangs of orgasm would begin to ebb. Oh, how it angered me! He was no less heartless than the Beasts of the Forest; the only difference was that His dispassion was rooted in conscience. Yes, His was a cold and callous conscience. He increased the distance between us to demonstrate to me what I was not, what I was incapable of. He counted on re-making me in His own image: pure, upstanding, asexual.

Increasingly, the Beasts squirming at my nether regions and my own convulsions started to resemble a grim form of gymnastics. I endeavored to void my thoughts of Him, to lose myself in the act. Enraged, stubborn, I dragged myself into the Forest, emptied of true desire. Under the Beasts' talons, I turned into a rotting piece of meat.

Finally, something odd happened: pleasure came only at the conclusion of the sexual act, once the Beasts that ran roughshod over me had fled. Their depredations were a ritual that laid the ground for the serenity that followed. The sight of blood, of my excoriated flesh, and the soft gusting breeze caressing my armpits soothed me. I retreated within myself. The only conduits for this introspection: my body and the dark.

Gradually, my nightly visits to the Forest tapered off.

GOD PROPOSED AN experiment: that we dispense with clothes and wander around the House naked. It was the only way, He said, for me to allay my feeling of artificiality once and for all. Having demanded that I sever my ties to nature, that I strive for perfection, He was now trying to be like me.

I agreed. What was I thinking? That my body would disarm him? As always, my husband was right. Nudity eradicated desire. After the initial shock, we just sat there, facing each other—He with His phantasmal wrinkled cock, I with my ass chafed by the wicker dining-room chair. A scene both unnerving and amusing.

"Let's end this," I said one day. "It's neither funny nor embarrassing. And it doesn't feel natural. What's the point? It's not teaching me anything."

"Wait and see," He replied. "It's a question of time. Human nature abandons you if you let it."

I hung on His every word. "What do You mean? Will I become immortal one day like You? Could that actually happen?"

Crossing His arms, He stared at me, sorrow in His eyes.

We discarded nudity and the unanswered questions of the body and turned to the issue of immortality. At least I did; He simply fell silent.

"But why? Why? If You love me, prove it. Change the rules. You could easily decree, 'God's wife will live forever.' What is stopping You? Why must I grow old and die? Then You'll have to go searching for another wife. Why are You so cruel?"

"You won't grow old if you renounce time. Nor will you die."

"I won't die?"

"Not in the way you think."

"Good grief. I'm tired of this nonsense."

Shrieking, gesticulating, completely beside myself, I trailed Him from room to room. "Shall I tell You why? Because You've tired of me! Yes, You've tired of me and won't admit it, not even to Yourself. Oh, You and Your spotless, saintly reputation! Yet here You are, gagging for an excuse to be rid of me. You can't wait to shed tears over my grave, to find someone else to soothe Your sorrow. Just say it! I'm right, aren't I?"

He turned and closed the door softly behind Him, leaving me alone. Ghost-like, He climbed the stairs and shut Himself away in His study. If God's wrath reveals itself in the repudiation of unrighteousness, then He was rejecting me. Yes, He wanted to wash His hands of me. Repentant, I would fall onto the couch and punch the pillows. Burying my face in them, I sobbed and sobbed. After each outburst I sought solace in books. My tears dried as I pored over Christian sermons: "God's wrath is not true. This is not the righteous anger of a God meting out justified punishment."

FOR A LONG time, my doubts concerning the nature of the world made me either cry or tremble with rage. Perhaps you find me self-indulgent or even hysterical, but put yourself in my position and think about the torment: I wake up, I sleep beside Him who holds the key to all knowledge. And all I ever get from Him is silence. "Again, you question without stopping to think," He would say. "All you care about is an impressive explanation."

When I wouldn't relent, my husband plucked philosophical or scholarly texts from the shelves. At first, they bored me. Little by little, in my solitude, I started leafing through them. I read Epicurus and Wittgenstein; the Gnostics and the Upanishads; the theory of relativity and the theory of probability; Henry David Thoreau's sojourn in the woods at Walden and the works of the philosopher who was his host there, Ralph Waldo Emerson. I read Marguerite Porete, a medieval mystic close to God's heart, who was unable to describe to us mere mortals what it felt like to become one with God: the experience was beyond words; God was the only one truly to understand her annihilation. (Naturally, I asked Him: Do You believe in the *longe propinquus*? Did You ever meet Marguerite? Was she one of Your wives? She was crazy about You—is that why You cherish her? Is that the kind of love You expect from me?" God refused to open His mouth.)

From these books, I retained random sentences, core doctrines, insignificant details that became meaningful to me. From Simone Weil, I preserved a strange wish: "To see a landscape as it is when I am not there." A similar line engrossed me in a Buddhist text: "There is a path to walk on, there is walking being done, but there is no traveler. There are deeds being done, but there is no doer." From the Latin texts, I absorbed the following proverb: "*Amare et sapere vix Deo conceditur.*" Which means, "It is scarcely granted to God to love and be wise." And speaking of proverbs, there was this Irish one: "When God created time, He created plenty of it."

In reading lines like these, the veil of my ignorance was torn asunder and within me something terrible and indefinable, something dark and cold, reared its head and rose slowly to the surface of my consciousness. But just as I was about to embrace it, to cling onto it as if it were a rock in a turbulent sea, that something crumbled, turned to dust. What a devastating defeat! A thousand times better never to have come close to understanding. A thousand times better to surrender to a life of common alms: unpaid bills, stacks of plates in the sink, mewling babies. I felt alone, terribly alone, powerless to fathom the mysteries of the cosmos, despite the fact that my companion was the perfect teacher. But perhaps that was to blame.

When I badgered Him about my dreams, He referred me to Synesius's treatise, *On Dreams*, which describes dreams as the space where we encounter the gods, or to Freud's *Interpretation of Dreams*. When I demanded incontrovertible proof, He picked up books on mathematical logic, pointing with His long, ghostly finger to Kurt Gödel's Incompleteness Theorems. According to those theorems, an arithmetical statement was neither provable nor disprovable, while the consistency of axioms could not be demonstrated within their own system. What did my husband mean by pointing this out? That unprovable statements are as true as those that are provable? Is it possible to have faith and freedom at the same time? Is this not the definition of madness, of uncertainty? And is it not this basic form of uncertainty that drives the devout towards their God? Naturally, that was not a question I could ask Him.

I made a mistake: I started reading books as if they held hidden answers. The pages He pointed to were replete with examples of love and blind submission; doubt, pleasure, and patience; the belief in progress and the disavowal of the world; electrons, photons, and prayers. Today, I know: there were no hidden messages; He was simply showing off His collection. Above all, my husband was an impassioned collector; a compiler of hypotheses about the workings of the world.

And so time passed, and so I aged. And as I aged, my needs changed, as did my questions. As did my disposition. I tired of struggling to understand. I stopped plying Him with questions. It happened, I remember, on our tenth wedding anniversary. I was twenty-seven years old and had asked thousands, millions of questions. We sliced a cherry cake, which only I ate. We opened a bottle of champagne, which only I drank.

"Have You noticed that I never ask You anything any more?" We clinked glasses. "Nothing personal, that is."

"You're maturing," He replied proudly, as if I were His child.

"And, for Your information, I no longer count the days. It feels silly to celebrate birthdays, anniversaries."

"Time is a convention," He observed, encouragingly. "It is defined in relation to movement and the intensity of the encompassing gravitational field."

"Don't talk to me like an astrophysicist. Tell me what time is to You."

"Time is what you make of it. Time simply is. It has no defined characteristics. It does not pass; it is not lost."

"What about space?"

And God, the great Surveyor, declared: "For the time being, you still feel the need to separate yourself from your surroundings;

to feel impermeable. Yes, it looks like you still need space."

He had told me at the very beginning: I had to relinquish my dependence on space. Gradually, the House, the Forest, the Angels, even God Himself, would all fade away. And, finally, I too would be gone.

AFTER I RELINQUISHED time, the Angels stopped playing soccer by the fence. Sundays ceased to be. The only things left to remind me of the lunar cycle, the moon's orbit, were my bloody tampons during my period. And as we all know, you lose it if you don't use it, so I also started forgetting the names of the months. There were no seasons; snow, heatwaves, floods; north or south. To accustom myself to timelessness, I read quantum theory. I imagined myself in a train carriage, traveling at a steady speed. I concentrated on drawing the curtains to block the view outside. Instantly, the train's forward momentum ground to a halt.

I also pored over Buddhist texts. Over Christian philosophers who claimed that the only way to eradicate the phenomenal world from one's senses—and thus liberate the boundlessness of the soul—was to acknowledge it as a product of human will. You see? I fought hard to banish the world from inside me, from around me, like the mystic, Porete. I had no rest. I asked myself the questions that He refused to answer. His silence was an insult; it mortified me. His offer of companionship was, in actual fact, a reign of terror. We did not doubt together, like blind animals. I was the only one beset by doubt. He simply knew. He wielded His wrath, His silence to impose His rules.

How did I come to this realization? When I decided to take notes from the books He provided. I wanted to jot down proverbs, arguments that intrigued me. And I wanted to draw, the way I used to. Naturally, my first step was to pray for paper and pencil. No pencil appeared. Trying to explain myself to the Angels, I pinched my thumb, index and middle fingers together and traced a garland in the air. The Angels stared at me curiously, clearly thinking I was trying to cross myself and that my arm refused to cooperate. Then, they turned to each other and engaged in that strange prattle of theirs. I was sure they

were discussing the Trinity. "No, no," I said. "Pencil. Pen-cil."
Frustrated, I went upstairs to my husband's Study.

I HAVE NOT yet told you about His Study. It is big, but because
of the shelves covering the walls, it is claustrophobic. Imagine
a round dome lined with books to the very top. Without a single decorative item. No paperknives, no bookmarks, no papers.
Only books, a black wooden desk, and His armchair, a deep
black bergère bare of cushions. Oh, yes, and a rope ladder for the
higher shelves. He calls it "Wittgenstein's ladder." Like the desk
or the armchair, it is there to throw dust in my eyes. What's the
likelihood of God needing a ladder to reach the highest shelves?

His books are scattered everywhere. He reads two or three
at a time and discards them wherever He happens to be. Even
though He is by nature meticulous and orderly, books bring out
something strange in Him: He rearranges them, and when they
no longer fit on the shelves, He stacks them on the floor. After
a while, the books on the floor find their way onto the shelves,
only for some of the books on the shelf to disappear. What does
He do with them? Does He give them away? To whom? Do the
Angels borrow them? Or, true to the eternal cycle of matter on
Earth, does He pulp them?

What are God's favorite subjects? Cosmology, philosophy,
anthropology, history of art (He devours art books). He pores
over studies of comparative religion and quantum mechanics.
He admires Spinoza for reverencing the universe and respecting
others' opinions; Kant for his notion of beauty as purposive without purpose; Nietzsche for positing that our survival on earth is
predicated on our ignorance; and Galileo for his nimble wit and
business acumen.

He treasures the pre-Socratic philosophers, especially
Xenocrates; Hegel; and, strangely, his great rival, Schelling. He
reads everything: from Origen of Alexandria and Lucretius, to
the Smalcald Articles and the *Formula Concordiae*. The texts of
the peripatetic monastic preacher, Vatsa, who rejected all means
of knowledge, take pride of place on His shelves. The Buddhist
sutras wedged alongside Wittgenstein and other neo-positivists

testify to what they all have in common: the rigor of their reasoning.

He is partial to texts that appear never to have been published and which He alone is responsible for salvaging from oblivion: *Celibacy* by Isidor of Ephesus; *On the Exercise of Freedom and the Creation of the Universe* by Ezidio Cerroti; *Zero* by Sued Ziadi; *God's Despair* by a certain O.B. Sanderson. In the manuscripts collected in the library, I discovered a multitude of scholars whose names I had not heard before. I have a well-founded suspicion (correct me, if I'm wrong) that these writers did not find a publisher for their work because their views were too extreme or heretical: Licinius, Jeremy Echt, Natalia Scarmotti, Phillip Cod. I also found some half-burnt manuscripts. Perhaps God plucked these out of the fires of the Inquisition with His very own hand. On the topmost shelves, I found Mayan hieroglyphs which, as far as I know, were destroyed by that zealot, Father Diego de Landa. There, too, are the Buddhist texts burned by the Turkish invaders of India in the eleventh century, as well as the Gnostic Gospels, the majority of which were systematically destroyed.

God finds His deniers amusing. He has dedicated an entire wall to them: from Diagoras of Melos to John Stuart Mill, Bakunin, Simone de Beauvoir, and Foucault. "I like people who fight for their ideas," He says.

What are some of God's least favorite things? Children's literature. He detests fairy tales for their didacticism and simplemindedness. Also, He is not a fan of what He describes as the absurdity of fiction and poetry. There are no novels, no collections of poetry in God's library. "I don't understand why they need to invent things that don't exist," He says. I'm baffled: Isn't that exactly what He did?

THAT DAY, I barged in without knocking to find Him poring over one of His favorites: Plato's *Timaeus*. (I find His obsession with reading about a place that pre-dates Him troubling. Does He long to return to the darkness of pre-History?).

I described my difficulties in summoning paper and pencil.

"There are no pencils here," He replied bluntly. "No fountain pens, no ballpoints, no computers, no paper. Also, no cameras. There's no need for documentation, for evidence."

Kneeling at His feet, I asked Him whether He trusted me.

"Trust is not the issue," He replied and extended His hand to pull me upright. "There's no need for histrionics."

"Please, listen to me. Why are you talking to me like this? Are you afraid I might betray You?"

He stared at me as if He could not believe His ears. "You? Betray me? What are you talking about?"

"Well, let's assume the worst. Let's say I write a tell-all about You. It's not as if it can't be done, right? Writers, even when they aspire to realism, often tell falsehoods. You were the one who taught me that. That's what writers do, isn't it? Fiction writers, I mean. In which case, I wouldn't necessarily be exposing You."

"That's not what I was thinking at all."

"Then what?"

"It's simple: writing has no place here. It bespeaks a fundamental disbelief in a moral order. Creation ought to be self-evident."

"But I don't want to create anything! I just want to jot down a few notes. At most, I might do a little sketching."

He rose from his armchair, casting me a look I wouldn't wish on anyone. "That's how it starts. With notes and sketches. Anything that echoes the conception of the Original Idea is strictly prohibited, understand? I want nothing to do with the devastation that started all this."

Anything that echoes the conception of the Original Idea? He had never spoken in such a personal vein before. He said He was concerned about my problems, my happiness. He listened to my demands, my stories, my dreams. It did not take any particular insight to understand that in speaking of the Original Idea, He was speaking about the creation of the world. It was the first time we had come so close to the truth. God was afraid.

"Don't ask me for pencil and paper again," He concluded perfunctorily.

That was the end of our conversation.

I had mentioned writing a tell-all. But isn't that exactly what

I'm doing? I don't know whether I'll finish this letter; whether I'll find a way to get it to you. Or whether a time will come when I'll be able to hand it to you, like a runner in a relay race passing the baton. We are human beings, aren't we? We seek knowledge. On the other hand, when you know what I know, you may not want to share it with anyone else. You may decide to lock yourself in a room or hide in a cave and bury the secret with you. It's up to you. As long as there are two of us.

There is madness in solitude, but community in two.

MY HUSBAND APPEARS out of nowhere. At midday, I look up from the dining table and there He is. Silently, He sits down opposite me. How I have missed Him! How I long to talk to Him, to tell Him everything! I even want to tell Him about the letter I am writing, but I know that such a revelation would be the beginning of the end. He avoids looking me in the eye; He pokes at His plate like a child playing with its food. What can I do? I too eat with my head lowered over my plate. I think of my mother, who always ate like that when my father was on shore leave. As if she had no neck, no face. As if she did not know how to sit straight, how to find something to talk about—she, who could talk so beautifully.

How did things come to such a pass? I, a good-hearted inno-cent, eager to accept and justify anything, have turned into a mis-trustful, cantankerous neurotic. And He, who was all light, has become vindictive, bitter, resentful, demanding, as hard as stone. I, too, retreat into myself. Only through silence will I regain His trust. I do not mind waiting. I have my writing.

And you.

WHAT DID I learn from God about the nature of world? What did I deduce from our conversations?

That there is no reason for the existence of the universe.

That the religious mind does not reason.

That occasionally it can be very worthwhile to shatter the cage of language and look at the world through the pure eyes of a infant untainted by words.

That life has no meaning; we are the ones who give it meaning.

And here, in a nutshell, is what my husband believes: theology and philosophy are tools for understanding the struggle between doubt and faith, tools for appeasing the heart. Religions exploit our spiritual vulnerabilities, preaching now forced solidarity, now bigotry. The literal reading of texts leads to fundamentalism. Deep down, He says, we are all alone.

Is He a misanthrope? At such times, where is His faith in the faith He demands of me? Don't such assertions on His part belie the fundaments of love? This is what I hint at whenever we broach such matters. With disarming sincerity, God admits that religions irk Him for formalist reasons: for their literal reading of allegory. "And what's wrong with allegory?" I protest. "It makes children of adults at a point in their lives when they have become cynical and heartless in so many ways. Isn't there something wonderful in the human urge to invent new ways of believing?" That's when He gets angry: "Myth is no replacement for faith! Don't you understand? We can't make a fiction of everything!"

Even the Bible is fiction to Him. That's why we didn't have a copy of it in our library (I write "our," the pronoun of established couples, the delusion of shared property). God is not swayed by either the realism and optimism of the Old Testament or the idealism and pessimism of the New. Both volumes, He says, for better or worse, coincide on the allegory of the Fall. They speak to two different spiritual inclinations in humanity: first, hope and fear; then, devastation, self-punishment, and the projection of responsibility onto the unknown. In God's words: Up until original sin, the world was consumed with the quest for a reason for being. Thereafter, with the quest for salvation.

When I finally read the Bible, I disagreed with Him. One day, I mean to tell Him: The God of the Bible—that merciful, impatient, ultra-virtuous, and rancorous God—is the spitting image of my husband. In the same way that statues in art books remind us what the body is capable of, so too the God of the Bible reminds us how small is the distance between despair and love.

I know because I see it in myself. I love, yet I trample on that love; I destroy the sacred compact of faith, the spousal privilege of privacy. If what is godly in me is this freedom—the protestations of conscience—then I am beginning to imitate God. The only meaningful difference between us is that, unlike Him, I want to narrate my story. I must get to the end. If I stop now, it would be akin to condemning both my husband and myself to burial under the drifting sands of biblical deserts while I sat by, with folded arms.

HE NO LONGER eats with me every day. Nor does He sleep in our bed. I leave it up to Him to decide the right time to talk about what has happened on our journey together, about everything I am about to tell you. I imagine He will say: "Forget everything I said." And I will be good, accommodating. I will listen until the end without protest or interruption. Then, I will say: "I cannot forget what You said, but I understand where You are coming from."

I try to make my way down to the dining room at my regular time, to take my usual stroll in the Forest before nightfall. Perhaps He would rather we met outside, at the foot of our tree. In my mind's eye, I see Him walking leisurely over the grass, coming toward me with a book tucked under His arm. Occasionally, overcome by nostalgia, I lie under the plane tree. He never comes.

It's all a big tangled mess in my head. As I wait for Him to appear, I wonder whether you will be the one to arrive instead. The more time passes, the more distant He becomes and the more you supplant Him as my interlocutor. However, I fear that I'm treating you the way He treats me. I speak, and expect you to abide by the compact of faith I offer. At the same time, I cannot hear any of the questions you may have. Do you know what I'm thinking? That perhaps He too, in all these years, only heard an indistinct cry, a muffled shriek from me, cloaking my true doubt. Perhaps at its heart, the problem is one of untuned frequencies.

FOR MANY YEARS, I was ignorant of the ban on pencils. It had no bearing on me. I was young and had so many other things to do: I flew; I walked on the water of the lake; I read; I offered my body with abandon, shameless as water. As I grew older, I remembered pencils.

I prayed for a pencil, my eyes to the heavens like the Christ in Auntie's icon. I became fretful, melancholic. I began to suffer acute pains in my womb, my breasts. Sometimes, it felt like a vise was clamping my temples, the nape of my neck. I lay on the bed, unable even to read. Angels applied cold compresses to my forehead. God visited morning and evening. He was always with me. He didn't begrudge me my tears and sighs.

"If You can't stand me any more, let's separate," I said one day.

He stroked my forehead. "Well, that day will come eventually," He replied.

To remind me of my mortality like that was a great indiscretion on His part. But I should also point out that He knows nothing of irony. Everything He says is utterly literal. In this unearthly abode of ours, His literalism could break bones.

Now that the period of great depression has passed, I don't know what to think about this "eventually" of God's. How old am I? The question has no value here. Time is manifest only relationally. In God's kingdom I cannot do human things with time: wait, dream, compare. Nevertheless, my wrinkles have grown deeper. The mirror at the hotel we ended up in during our travels told me so. Every day I trace them with my fingers. My hands are covered with bulging veins, the skin parched and thin.

So yes, a long time must have passed since I married Him. He no longer looks old to me. We must resemble a couple from those bygone eras when the husband always had ten to twenty years on his wife. We have had a good life—the only exception: the unfortunate events at the end of our journey. At times, I cannot understand where my bad temper comes from. Before me, crystal clear, I see the life I would have lived had I not met Him: Auntie would have died one day (perhaps it has already happened) and my torments at the hands of my brother would have been carried on by someone else, a husband perhaps. Oh, yes, life would have trampled all over us: financial troubles, children, discord and disagreement, friends' untimely deaths.

God watches over me; He talks to me with tenderness; He

keeps me company at the table. He picks at the fruit on the platter in order to endow our meetings with meaning. "Don't swallow your food without first chewing it properly!" He admonishes. His every sentence, a pretext for a philosophical discussion: from unchewed food we move to greed, from there to rage and boredom. My husband is at ease with abstraction. In comparison to Him, I am like a first-year philosophy student. Yes, we live in harmony. We talk and argue just like any other middle-aged couple. What then is this thing that crushes my soul? Cruelty, I would say, if I were being malicious.

Writing. My need to tell you this story without anyone correcting me. Without anyone interrupting me.

MOTHER USED TO say that reading books is for those who can't do. On our bookshelves sat an icon of St. Nicholas, protector of the seafarer, and an encyclopedia with gold lettering on its spine. No-one ever opened it. At school we were asked to write essays that espoused the solidarity of nations. I find it difficult to write in a way that is neither aestheticized nor didactic. It's as if people do it on purpose: they start by telling the truth, then, in the middle of a sentence, they freeze.

Since I started writing, I have felt as if I am committing a sin. No longer do I observe my thoughts as if they were flies, flitting whimsically from my knee to my elbow and back again. Now, I cling to ideas, I spin them into conjecture and hypothesis. I poison my life with them. But my husband also has His own hypotheses and conjectures—I know that now.

Everything I know, I learned after my serious illness. Being ill is actually the ultimate cry for attention. This is how it goes: you get sick, and if you survive, you learn. I crawled into bed and couldn't get back up. The Angels' cries seemed to come from far away—as if someone had stuffed them all in a pot and covered it with a lid.

I don't know if there is a name for my illness. It came suddenly, in powerful waves that pulled me under. I did not have the strength to get out of bed; even turning from left to right was an ordeal. All I could do was lie on my back and stare up at a single spot on the ceiling. Shifting my attention to another spot was too much for me. My mind was completely numb, and I observed that numbness with curiosity and sadness. My priority was to lie as still as possible and to black out the areas that refused to succumb. A battle of self against self in which victory meant the unconditional surrender to nothingness.

I could not get up to eat. Every day, late in the afternoon, the Angels brought me vegetable broth to drink through a straw. Kneeling at my bedside, they prayed for me, stroking my hair, whispering "*krrrl*," in resignation. Every time God came through the door, He asked the same question: "How do you feel?" I did not have the strength to answer. Finally, He stopped asking. He would burrow under the sheets and switch off the light. One day, I begged Him to sleep somewhere else. I had difficulty sleeping and the slightest sound would wake me up.

I started dreaming about my own death. How can I put it? I longed for a tranquil parting, a serene and gradual sinking and decline. I must have been mumbling to myself, describing the scene of my death, because at the edges of my vision two Angels leaped to their feet and started shrieking. As if a lion had charged into the room, that's how loud and frantic were their shrieks. God appeared out of nowhere. The Angels ushered Him into a corner and huddled with Him there, gesticulating, whispering. Agonizingly, I propped myself up and then fell back against the pillows.

He stood over me, His ghostly hands on my cheeks. I clung to those hands, the ethereal fingers, the wrists. "Here," He said. "Here! Look at me! Don't close your eyes! You must not reject life! What do you need to be happy? Your wish is my command. Ask for whatever you want. Don't hold back. Do you want to return to the world? Is that what you want?"

Everything went dark. God and the Angels behind Him were swallowed in a black vortex.

THE BED WAS thronged with Angels. They plied me with compresses and soothing drinks. Like a mortal man, God stood a little to the side, watching in bewilderment. Now I know why:

my abandonment reminded Him of His own despair when He withdrew to His lair after the creation of the world. But I'm getting ahead of myself.

"I'm not to blame for this," I whispered with difficulty. "It's got me in its clutches . . . I will try . . . I will tell you."

He waved the Angels out of the room. Face resplendent, He sat on the edge of the bed like when we first met. Only the apprehension in His eyes betrayed all that we had shared.

"Come closer, please," I whispered with all the strength I could muster. "We love Him, because He first loved us."

"I do not doubt your love," He replied sternly, stroking my hair.

I did not ask to go back. I wished neither for the earthly life that belonged to me, nor for a dignified death. No. I asked Him to take me Lands away, on a journey to the world.

In my weakened condition, I needed my husband at my side. Yes, it's true, I dreamed of the looseness of freedom, of breaking the chains. But life is one thing, and dream another entirely. Alone in the world? Impossible! I think it was Kierkegaard who said: Repetition and recollection are the same movement, except in opposite directions. Recollection moves backward, whereas repetition is a recollection that moves forward, like the creation of the world. This reflection speaks straight to my heart: "If God had not willed repetition, the world would not have come into existence. Either He would have followed the superficial plans of hope or He would have retracted everything and preserved it in His recollection. This He did not do. Therefore, the world continues, and it continues because it is repetition." I yielded to repetition, to habit. To God's plan.

"Let it be," He said and His terrible eyes seared right through me, like a lightning bolt. But I did not dwell in the light of those eyes, which, as you now know, show me everything I covet, everything I fear. The veil was finally torn: I could see that my plight pained my husband, that He loved me. He preferred to lose me rather than let me lose myself in despondency and despair. His divine will bent before my nostalgia for the world.

I did not betray Him, nor He me. We were still together.

I SPENT THE entire night mopping. I concentrated on a small area under the desk in my study, going over it with the mop again and again, afraid to let it dry. In my dream, it seemed to do so almost instantly, and I had to work hard to keep the surface shiny and wet.

The mop strings looked like a woman's hair. After wringing it in the bucket repeatedly, I realized the hair was mine. An oxidized mirror hung across from me as I mopped. I glanced at myself: my head was completely bald. This sight did not disturb me; on the contrary, I continued my work with renewed vigor. My only concern was that the shininess under the table legs not be lost. In my dream, the meaning of life was that gleam on the floor. The lustrous surface attested—or so it seemed to me—to something about the person mopping. To something about me.

When I was little, I dreamed I could fly. When I learned to fly for real, I stopped dreaming of the impossible. At first, I told Him about my dreams. But as you probably know by now, God is no fan of an unbridled imagination. I stopped telling Him about my dreams. Finally, I even stopped dreaming. When my husband agreed to travel the world with me, I dreamed the mop dream. I kept it to myself. I now reveal it to you.

Our plan was to wait until I got stronger. In my dream, I was starting to prepare.

HE WAS WEARING a white linen suit and a straw hat with a black silk band, I a white dress with a butterfly pattern, embroidered years ago. Over my shoulders, I'd thrown a shawl I'd knitted. In my hand, I held a bag big enough to hold everything we might need. He had explained that during the journey, we would be dependent on the physical world, that we would eat real food. I would not be able to fly or control the weather. We would have to abide by the laws of life on Earth. This both pleased and frightened me.

"How do I look?" I asked.

"Very beautiful," He answered. "I like the butterflies." And then, in a lower voice, "How about me?"

Was He teasing, or was He trying on mortality for size? I believe that what had just happened to Him was without precedent. He had been forced to shed His divine implacability. Doubt, fury, ambivalence had all brought Him closer to understanding human vulnerability, had forced His decision to taste mortality for the sake of a mortal. And on whom had God decided to bestow this great mercy, this unfathomable favor? Me.

"Why are you crying? I only asked how I look."

"Wonderful," I said and fell into His arms. His body had become denser. I drew back to get a better look. Skin flushed with vigor, pale purple veins pulsing. And bones, too, soft and supple, like a frog's or a bird's. I couldn't get enough of Him. Ears, eyes, lips. I was burning with desire to see teeth, stomach, perhaps even what lay a little lower.

"It's a miracle!"

"No, it's not a miracle!" He grabbed my wrists, His eyes stern, piercing. "When will you have done with this ridiculous religious literalism!"

"No, no, I meant marvelous. A miracle as in a marvel, in other words . . . marvelous. Really! I meant that You're now ready for our trip."

He sighed, "As far as is humanly possible."

I had almost ruined everything with my inappropriate choice of words. I basked in His arms. A line from one of St. Bernard's sermons came to mind: "No one has ascended to heaven except he who descended from heaven." I promised myself that that was exactly what I would do. Holding my husband tightly by the hand, I would descend and then re-ascend.

PURGATORIO

The best one can hope for as a human is to have a relationship
with that emptiness where God would be if God were available,
but God isn't.

Anne Carson

WE ENDED UP strolling along a path in a park thrumming with people. He led the way; I followed. Dragon kites slashed the skies. Over the grass, under the trees, children chased after each other. The sun tore through the clouds to splash on their hair.

"Good Lord," I whispered.

He gave me a curious glance. I could barely contain myself: Look at the sun, the clouds! Look at the people: all shining silhouettes, pulsing veins, rippling muscles. Look at their animal vitality—how they hug, how they eat. How they huddle in a corner talking to each other. Look, look! Some walk alone, hands plunged deep in their pockets; others snap pictures. Look at the groundskeeper over there, at the long, slow swish of his broom. Look at that man smoking—it's been years since I last saw someone smoking. Where is that scrum headed in such haste? Schoolboys—I know that gait well. There's a woman holding an umbrella to shield her face from the sun. Do you see that lot with the beers over there? Soon, they'll be completely drunk. Most of all, I enjoy the girls walking in pairs. You can almost feel the buoyancy, the vigor of their limbs. Sweat, like dew, at their napes.

"I'm fine. Nothing's on my mind," I explained. "Nothing, except this."

"Isn't this what you wanted?"

"Exactly. This."

The park was large, sprawling, a maze of winding paths and avenues. Ours got narrower and narrower. I wanted to switch to the main avenue, but was hesitant to mingle with the teeming crowds, to walk among them. What if they turned to me? What if they proclaimed: "Here she is, the woman who forgot how to live among her own!"? To what race did these people belong? What language were they speaking? Their mouths spat out rapid bursts of words.

He waved me ahead, then trailed behind. He was worried about me, and with good reason: human voices, dogs' barks, children's footsteps echoed within me as if I had the power to amplify sound. Were people staring at me? Was there something strange in my demeanor? In my bearing?

Calm down, I admonished myself. You are a human being amongst other human beings. No one is staring. No one knows how long you've been gone or why. No one knows who that is beside you. You look like father and daughter. The picture of normality. He, an older gentleman wearing a straw hat, and you, gawking at everything like a woman traveling for the first time. Two tourists in a distant land. Yes, tourists. Everything new to you.

As I WRITE, I am wracked with a terrible nostalgia for the world. For smells, tastes, the friction of bodies. For night and rain streaming aslant under the glow of streetlamps. For dawn and its cadence of voices and crates scraping across sidewalks. For the hum of air-conditioning, the bleat of cars, the mewl of babies. For the great blessing that is sound—all of it.

At first, I couldn't stop staring at clocks, at wall calendars. Why did I allow myself to get taken in like that? Once again, I started counting down the days and hours. I became reacquainted with words like "weekend," "weekday," "autumn." Ah, Tuesday, I'd think (that's when we used to have beans for dinner); Thursday (ballet class!); Sunday afternoon (in front of the television). At every street corner, God tugged my hand:

"You're dawdling again!"

I miss the little things the most: tire tracks through muddy snow; the smell of grass; the shack with the couple breaking eggs for an omelet. Their empty, still sizzling pan. I can see its bare roundness, the smoky finale.

The human world was—how to explain? Worn. Endowed with the dignity lent by wear. Some nights, with my nose against the windowpane, I stared at the deserted weave of overpasses. Why didn't the sight recall the stillness of God's kingdom? Perhaps because every road would be teeming again shortly; the roads were merely resting before resuming their burden: humans and their vehicles. If roads have an inner life, then during the wee hours they must surely contemplate the hardness of their lot: the ravages, the wear and tear of traffic. Whereas back in our world—how does the poem put it? "There is a path to walk on, there is walking being done, but there is no traveler."

ON A PLATFORM in the middle of the park, couples, young and old, were waltzing, wearing clothes of a bygone era—chintz dresses, striped shirts. Music blasted through speakers. He huddled under the shade of a tree on the margins. I rushed to the stage, hungry to see.

A man in sandals and linen pants bowed to me. I turned to God, who nodded reassuringly. I gave my hand to this stranger and with a light tug he drew me towards him. My hand in his: the feel and funk of humanity. The smell of grass and cigarettes on his fingers as he showed me how to do a back turn. Preposterous! After such a lengthy absence to be dancing with a man I'd never met before and would never see again. God was following our every move. Never had I felt He belonged to me as much as He did that moment, as I spun in the hands of a stranger. I was finally flirting with my husband again. Pretending not to notice Him. But dancing only for Him.

As soon as the song ended, I rushed back to Him.

"God, it's so hot!" I dabbed the back of my neck with a tissue from my bag.

"You dance beautifully."

"Have You ever danced?"

"Can you imagine me dancing?"

"Of course. You're capable of anything."

"Anything?"

"Yes, and if You love me, You must dance with me."

"If I love you, I love you. It goes without saying."

He laughed. I laughed, too. I had forgotten how much we liked to laugh like that, without any reason. Teasing each other, the same as we had in the early years of our marriage. Once we returned to the path, our laughter ebbed. We read the tags on tree trunks: *Nerium Indicum. Salix Babylonica L. Sapium Sebiferum. Torreya grandis.* On a bridge, we leaned over the railing to peer at a lake covered in lily pads. Large, green, flowerless orbs. Scores of goldfish sparkling in the muddy water, making their separate ways through the crowded murkiness.

"What's the matter? You're not crying, are you?"

"The water is filthy. And there are so many fish. Look, they barely fit!"

He looked at me curiously.

"Not only the fish. What about the people, the trees, everything?"

Children blowing soap-bubbles, high-pitched cries, pungent food odors. I stumbled and fell on my face in the middle of the bridge.

"Don't worry, I'm all right. It's just that . . ."

Anxiously, He hovered over me.

"I'm fine. I just need to rest a while on the grass."

With His help, I picked myself up and dusted off my dress. Oh, the strangeness of His body, His smell. What did God smell like? Crushed chamomile.

I sat down on the shawl I'd spread on the ground. He settled at my side. Silently, we watched the playing children. I lay back, cheek on elbow. The earth actually smelled of earth. A woman wearing flip-flops passed in front of me, a baby strapped to her chest. She was patting its back to make it burp.

"Incredible how naturally everything happens," I remarked.

"What did you expect? They're simply living their lives."

"Yes, but they have no inkling of a wider order, another framework, do they? They talk to each other as if it were the most natural thing in the world."

"It is."

"To them. Whereas I cannot get over the fact that people have names, professions, children."

My husband turned to look elsewhere—He always does when I bring up children. I followed His gaze. A girl wearing black pajamas was leading two men, also in black, in a series of martial arts postures. They held themselves upright, torsos slack, bending their knees as if about to sit down. Abruptly, capriciously, they shifted their weight onto one leg, then the other. Their arms traced in the air the contours of a large ball. Periodically, they pulled it to their chests before pushing it as far away as they could.

He patted my hair. "Don't try to take it all in at once. It is impossible." He patted me the way mother had, with abnegation. I dozed.

When I opened my eyes, God was doing tai-chi. Standing tall, in step with the girl and the two men, He plucked at the strings of a ghostly instrument. Together, the four of them alternated between shifting their weight onto their forward leg, as if pinning down the hem of an invisible tunic, then walking backwards slowly, heavily, like astronauts. I sat up and rubbed my eyes. Wasn't He worried the grace of His movements might give Him away? Was I the only one who could see He was wreathed in light? Then, I thought to myself: What if He becomes interested in other people? What will I do without Him?

But no-one was paying Him any special attention. While I was asleep, His features had adapted to the environment: cheekbones imperceptibly higher; nose flatter, as if the bone had been broken; eyes deeper in their sockets; face rounder. He looked part Asian.

In the middle of the park, God was practicing martial arts. My heart leapt at the thought that perhaps He was doing it for me: to dance the dance I had requested of Him. I was the only one in the entire world who knew who He was. And I still hadn't turned innocence into intent. I had not yet started my letter to you.

WE HAD LUNCH in the park's only restaurant. Chinese characters covered the menu. He ordered; speaking fluently, joking a little with the waiter. Once we were alone again, I asked Him if He spoke all the world's languages.

"I think you know the answer. Sometimes you ask things only to keep conversation going."

"What's wrong with that? What should we do? Sit here in silence until the food arrives?"

"Preferably, yes."

I smoothed the white tablecloth. It had been pressed by human hands. The sound of ringing cutlery came from the tables next to ours.

Rice and vegetables. Steamed asparagus. Green tea, and warm towels for our hands. I counted three dumplings in a bamboo basket. We devoured the food—even God polished His plate. When the time came to pay, He handed me a manila envelope stuffed with crisp bills. He told me to keep the rest for our other necessities.

"What's wrong?"

"It's a wad of paper. Just paper."

He glanced at me, eyes bright with curiosity.

"It's been many years since I held money in my hands."

At the door, the waiter bowed. God responded with a deep bow of His own. I was bowled over by His humility, His adaptability.

I could not tear myself away from that park. The warm solidity of my husband's arm. I could not stop holding onto Him, like a newlywed on her honeymoon. We walked and walked, resting occasionally in outdoor pavilions. Discovering rippling lakes, winding bridges, gilded spiderwebs.

When the sound of music reached my ears, I dragged Him towards it. Towards exotic musical instruments: stringed flutes, round-bodied lutes. The vocalist was standing, singing with eyes shut, fist clenched tight around the microphone. A short pause to listen before we moved on.

"Let's go," He said finally. "We have to find a place to sleep tonight."

Tonight: a word new to our shared vocabulary. Tomorrow, today, yesterday: all words I had long forgotten.

WE WOUND UP at a tall block of rental apartments near the park. God surrendered our passports to the reception clerk. Standing on tiptoes, I tried to glimpse His signature in the guest book. A work of art in ideograms.

"You are curious," He murmured.

"Very."

He asked me what I thought I would discover from a fake document with a fake signature.

"May I see my passport at least?"

He gave it to me. It unnerved me to read my name and surname, to see a photograph no-one had taken. "Better You hold onto it," I said.

Our apartment was small and grimy, the towels threadbare, the window-handle black with air pollution. Carefully, I wiped it off with a tissue. We were on the thirtieth floor. At this height, the entire web of city spread out beneath us. A railroad bridge, highways, buildings as tall as ours, all covered with neon advertising. The sun sank behind the skyscrapers. I leaned out of the window to watch the dying light.

"Careful!" God cried.

"Why? If I fall, You'll save me, won't You?"

"I've told you time and time again. I'm not a magician."

There was a mirror in the bathroom. For a long time, I stared at my face—my eyes, my nose, my greying hair. "I'm the spitting image of my mother! I have the same wrinkles around my eyes as she did."

"No," He said.

"You wouldn't know. I'm the spitting image of mother. It's been years since I've seen the parting in my hair. Even our parting is the same!"

"What do you mean? A parting is a parting: it parts the hair in two."

That first night we spent in the world, my husband did not read in bed. He switched off the light and the world around us evaporated. Once again, it was just the two of us. I wonder now whether He believed that my return to the world would heal me. And what about me? Was I still hankering for the drama of salvation? Did my love for Him somehow fall short? Perhaps what I called love was mere vanity: my gloating over His achievements, the mystery of His identity as we traveled incognito amongst strangers? What if my love was simply a reflex, a response to what I perceived as the honor He was doing me? In the sheltering darkness, I wondered: Was my devotion to my parents contingent on their deaths; my devotion to God, on His choice of me?

As always, He slept at the very edge of the bed. Sliding across, I nestled up against Him. Again, He felt airier, as if He'd lost the directions to corporeality. After wearing a body all day for me, He had abandoned Himself to sleep, wreathed only in His divinity. Our journey was an ordeal for Him, too. I was His wife. It was my duty to support Him.

That first night back in the world, I could not sleep. I got up and walked round and round in circles by the foot of the bed. Then, I tiptoed to the window. Through the curtains, something beckoned. I lifted the fabric and looked out: an inhuman, livid light bathed the skies. I had forgotten how the moon frightened me. How it sickened me.

The next morning, I walked out of the bathroom wrapped in my robe and found Him sitting on the edge of the bed. He was glaring angrily at the skyscrapers outside our window. The sky was low and grey. The din of traffic echoed from below.

"Let's go back to the park, shall we? It will be quiet there. And then let's hop on the subway and see where it takes us. Are there any museums around here? I haven't been to one since I was little! Do you know what I like about museums? People are so quiet. You can people-watch in peace."

"Museums are dead," He said. "I don't see the point in all those collections."

I almost blurted that He was the consummate collector. But I kept my mouth shut.

I packed money, tissues, and the key to our room in my bag. With the exception of my hand, which He held onto only with an effort, God preferred to keep His hands free. I took His arm.

It was solid again, vibrant with green veins. Rife with life.

TODAY, HE SUDDENLY appears in the dining room. He hunches over His plate—a specter pretending to chew and digest its food. One moment, I am there, at His side, and the next I am locked in the laundry room trying to recall the human body He wore during our trip. I want to tell you about His veins, the mirage of pulsing blood at His temples.

"What's wrong?"

"Nothing." He shrugs, as if conversation is not worth the trouble.

"We need to talk."

"When the time comes," He snaps, without looking at me.

"What do You do all day? Are You thinking about things?"

He smiles wryly, His head still bowed. "You might say that."

"You are neither here nor there."

"You ought to accept others for what they are."

"But You just aren't. You are nowhere."

"Learn to deal with nowhere, then." Without another word He pushes His chair back, gets up, and leaves the dining room.

He's right. I have trouble accepting Him because I have trouble idealizing anything. And I have trouble idealizing, because I know too much.

DURING OUR SECOND day in the world, we walked across the park, leaving babies, kites, singers, and couples behind us. Hand in hand, we strayed down a main road. The chaos! People spitting in the middle of the road, heading straight at us on their bicycles and motorbikes, in their cars. God had a sixth sense when it came to dodging disaster. As soon as He heard a honk, He stepped aside, dragging me with Him.

It was almost noon. A suffocating wind enveloped us. "Look at that child piddling by the side of the road! Look at that lot over there devouring a strange looking kebab—I wonder what's in it?" "Fried mice," He replied, and I roared with laughter. "Mice! Come on!"

We took the subway. God grasped the hand strap; I held onto

Him. A scrum of girls hemmed us in. Not caring if they bumped up against us, heedless of whether they trod on our toes. His eyes lingered on the girls, on their ebony hair, a little longer than I cared for. Giggling, they had Him surrounded. My husband could not resist telling a joke. Their laughter made me want to pull their hair out.

We got off at a station in a far quieter district and found ourselves in an open-air market selling teapots, agate jewelry, toy soldiers, and statuettes of oriental gods. I remembered the feeling of wanting something for its own sake, for no particular reason; of money changing hands; of coming into ownership of an object. By the time we left the market, I was carrying incense, a knitted shawl, a Buddha's head carved in wood.

"What's that for?"

"I have no idea," I replied frankly. "I like its dangling ear lobes."

Behind the flea market lay the bird market. Crested parrots and exotic birds peered at us from their cages, screeching angrily, pecking at water in porcelain bowls. The further we walked, the greater the confusion. Squatting women de-shelled turtles to make soup. Fish floundered in empty bowls. Molting chickens and ducks juddered in their crowded cages. A customer pointed at a chicken and one of the women grabbed it by the neck and held it upside down. Grasping the thrashing feet, she cut its throat with a pen-knife. Blood spurted onto the sidewalk.

"Take me away from here," I said. "I can't watch this."

"Of course you can. You just don't want to."

Plucking and smiling, baring black teeth, the woman with the bloody hands chatted with her customer. Turning to God, they said a few words.

He silently nodded. When I glanced at Him, His face was empty.

Still silent, we hastened away, my damp dress clinging to me. His clothes were dry and unwrinkled, as if He had a cooling mechanism hidden under His voluminous shirt.

"Are you thirsty?" He asked. "Let's go and get something to drink."

"Let's get away from here first. I want to get that woman out of my head."

A HULKING COMPLEX of shopping malls dominated the horizon up ahead. I plucked at his sleeve.

"Do you really want to go there?"

"Didn't you say you wanted something to drink? I'm sure they have air-conditioning."

Cloud Nine: the name of the mall. Nine floors, each packed with hundreds of shops: clothing, makeup, food, and drink. A supermarket occupied the basement, along with stalls selling confectionary, stationary, spectacles, underwear. God was aghast. I had never seen anything like it, either.

We found an empty bench in a juice shop. Highschool and university students came and went, earbuds in their ears. They sprawled on benches, tapping maniacally at their iPhones.

"There were no cellphones when I was growing up," I remarked, sipping my juice through a straw.

"I know."

"If we were late to an appointment, no one waited. That's why we weren't late."

"That makes sense."

"We used to write letters by hand. When we were done, we licked the envelope. The glue smelled horrible."

"Did you write letters often?"

I told him about the letters I'd written to my parents after they died. About scrawling their names on envelopes I then buried in the cemetery. Deep in the soil, next to their graves. "Dear mother, don't forget me." "Dear father, do you miss the sea?"

"How romantic," He said.

I stared at Him, in bewilderment.

"Yes," He repeated. "Sending letters like that, in the blind hope that they will reach their destination, is a romantic gesture."

"No, it's a gesture of faith," I corrected Him. "They were sent in the faith that they would reach their destination."

We had left the juice shop and were riding the escalators.

"Why do you get angry whenever you talk about faith?"

"You demand it of others, but You don't know what it is."

"I am faith," God said. "Therefore, you are angry at me."

"Yes, because I live by Your side."

"And what is so terrible about that?"

"Don't you understand? Everything is always just beyond my grasp. And I am doomed to invent. To believe everything I invent."

His eyes narrowed. "Doomed to invent . . ." He repeated. "There is nothing more dangerous. From the very first, I asked you to relinquish your desire for understanding, in other words for invention. Look around you: what exists is what you see. What else do you need?"

We had reached the top floor. The whorls of stairs and railings beneath us looked like a diagram of concentric eggs. I leaned over to get a better view.

He shouted. "Are you crazy! Don't lean so far!"

"I'm human. I crave a little danger!"

Again the struggle with a familiar doubt: If I fell, would He save me?

GOD IS SCARED of heights. During the first throes of Creation, He invented mountains to shelter His beloved trees from the violent winds that threatened to uproot them. During the Second Coming, He began to see in the mountains' peaked outlines a symbol of life's ups and downs. Cityscapes replace mountains with skyscrapers, scaffolding, stairs of every kind. To use a metaphor: mountains are unbearable burdens, elusive goals, irresolvable problems. I also have a religious metaphor: mountains are as immovable and impassive as my husband. In God's kingdom there are no heights, no anguish. With no horizon, with no view, we find ourselves in the ideal environment for utter equanimity.

I am now sailing into troubled waters, but there's no way around it: I believe that God's sojourn amongst humanity became embroiled in the mysteries of mountains. My husband began to suffer from vertigo. By the third evening, His ears were ringing. We requested a different room, and were moved to a larger apartment with a foyer on the third floor.

I'm worried you might be starting to find my secretiveness irritating. But if I blurted out everything at once, would you believe me? To expect you to absorb all this information in one sitting would be too much, don't you think? As you read, I would like you to retain, in equal measure, both your sense of time and a reverence for the present moment. Time might just be our salvation.

I LONGED TO visit a place of worship. After the Cloud Nine and the hordes of young people armed with smartphones, I missed the contemplativeness I was accustomed to in the House and the Forest.

We wound up at a temple built on a large platform. Intricately carved wooden parapets rose from the gold-plated roof. Covered walkways dotted with bald-headed monks linked the back gardens.

"May I pray?"

"As you wish," He replied.

I kneeled at a pew by the main shrine. Above me loomed a golden Buddha wreathed in candies, incense paper, apples. Bowing my head, I prayed to a God above God. I begged that my husband refrain from looking at other women. Before leaving my pew, I reached out to snatch a strawberry jelly candy. God was reading inscriptions a few steps away, and I went and put it in His hand. He had taken a liking to candy of late.

"That was an offering."

"Exactly, an offering to You. It's Yours."

He laughed. A handful of worshippers turned to stare at us.

UPON LEAVING THE temple we ran into a couple of students. With great warmth, they addressed God. I remember thinking: there must be something about Him that inspires trust. They spoke in English, the girl making broad, sweeping gestures. She was wearing beautiful linen pants, as unwrinkled as my husband's. Fortunately, God did not seem to notice her. The boy asked me if He was my husband and how we had met. I told him that He'd saved me from a flood when I was very young.

The student replied: "You're still young. Your skin is like velvet."
At length and adapting it to the rhythms of a regular romance,
I told the story of our meeting.

"Would you like some tea? I know an excellent place for the
traditional tea ceremony," the student proposed.

"No, we have to be going," God replied, rather curtly.

I clung to His arm. "Please, it's been so long since I've been
around people. They seem so nice, so polite . . ."

His eyes bored right through me. "As you wish," He said. I
forged ahead with the two students; He lagged behind. As we
mingled with the crowds, they pointed out the sights.

"Is it far?" I asked.

"No, we're almost there," the girl replied.

Sure enough, we were soon walking down a dark alleyway and
climbing the chipped marble stairs that led to a large, empty hall.
A woman with a limp served us green tea. The young man, eyes
averted, kept fidgeting, crossing and re-crossing his arms. The
young woman excused herself and fled to the bathroom.

"What's going on?" I asked my husband.

"Wait and see."

Our continued chatter no longer brought me pleasure, only
dread. The bill shortly arrived, in a small wooden box. A grotesquely inflated sum. The student's eyes turned nasty as I pulled
the manila envelope out of my bag. I counted the money—it
was not enough.

"No problem," the young man interjected hurriedly. "They
take credit cards. We're just students without a penny to our
names."

"We don't have any cards," God replied, with a scowl. "That's
all you're getting."

The limping woman whisked the envelope from my hands
and vanished. The students claimed they were running late.

God gave them a look I wouldn't wish on anyone. "The
weather's about to change," He declared. "You're going to need
umbrellas."

PENNILESS, WE WERE could take neither a cab nor the subway.

We walked for a long time in the rain. Rainwater pooled in the brim of God's hat. Every so often, without saying a word, He'd take it off, pour out the water, and put it back on again. The rain turned to hail, pelting our necks, backs, arms. I will never forget that deluge; my husband's leisurely gait. I wondered—I still do—whether it was all His doing. Whether it was His way of punishing the students for their deceit and me for my naiveté.

Wet, weary, we arrived at our apartment. The entire floor reeked of cigar smoke.

"That's no cigar," He said. "It's wormwood, used for heat therapy."

"Heat therapy?"

"Yes, they say it's a good way to increase vitality."

"Really?"

"I don't know. I've never had a problem with vitality."

I looked at Him closely: He was in good spirits. I was the wet and weary one.

Back in our room, He handed me another manila envelope.

"Be more prudent this time," He said

THE DOCTOR AND his assistant were wearing white uniforms. They had us lie down on two hard tables for massage and heat therapy. The doctor took care of God, while his assistant turned to me. At first, his rub was gentle, but soon it turned into long, hard strokes along the bones. How strange to feel a human touch! At the end, the assistant clenched his hands into fists and turned to knead the soles of my feet. There was little difference between my body and a bag of firewood.

Lying face down, my husband translated for me. The assistant said that my heart was afire (I imagined a heart smoldering in a furnace). God explained that this was a local turn of phrase meaning great emotion, a restless spirit. The heart, He continued, is a domineering organ, in charge of shielding the soul. As He talked, the assistant stuck needles in my palms and belly. The heavy odor of wormwood leaves sent me to sleep.

When I awoke, God had risen from the adjacent table and was gazing out of the window.

"What did the doctor say about You?"

He turned with an elusive smile. "He said that everything is exactly where it should be."

"EVERYTHING IS EXACTLY where it should be."

Was God pulling my leg? During our journey, He often talked about His incarnation with a mix of self-mockery and weary magnanimity.

"Wait and see."

"The weather's about to change. You're going to need umbrellas."

"I've never experienced anything like it."

"Be more prudent this time."

"I've never had a problem with vitality."

This is what I think: the same as I had missed life in the world, He now missed the affairs of divinity, whatever they might be. He betrayed His nostalgia in stray sentences, but mainly through His silence, despite my attempts to combat it with humor.

"If you visit a garage, it doesn't mean you're a car, right? So why does stepping inside a church make you a Christian?"

He would smile, but in the end His quiet melancholy prevailed. Had He grown bored of the world already? Was He longing to return? I don't know. I had no sense of where He was at, for He was where I was not. Our being apart—He there, I, here—was the condition of our being together.

More and more often, He went out alone. Apprehensive about the girls and their ebony hair, I trailed Him one day to the entrance of a large international bookstore. He darted down the main aisle, pulled a book off a shelf, and began reading furtively, as if He were doing something shameful. I watched through the window: every now and then, He looked up, glanced around. When He left, I went inside. I crossed the paper goods section , lingering to leaf through notebooks, sniff erasers, test the sharpness of pencils on the tips of my fingers. I had no trouble finding the book He had been reading: *Don Quixote* by Cervantes.

God had started reading fiction. Did that mean He didn't dislike it? Or had it become His earthly drug of choice?

THE FOLLOWING DAY, we set off for the nearest town on the river. I wanted to travel, to see something new, and my husband raised no objections. As usual, He led the way to the bus station. We bought bananas and candied ginger for the trip. We sat across from each other on an old, dirty bus whose floor was littered with sunflower seed husks. Through the window, we watched the skyscrapers, the bridges, the noise barriers roll by. We munched our ginger and before we knew it, we had left the city behind. A child tugged at his father's pants. The man got up, led the child to the bus steps, and pulled down his shorts. The child watched the thin stream trickle over the grooved metal. I looked away as he peed.

"They don't hide anything here," God said.

Our journey ended in the middle of a large square. I was suddenly reeling with exhaustion. I don't know if it was real exhaustion or the result of the smells, the din, the southerly wind that had been blustering since the morning. We climbed aboard a cycle rickshaw and the driver took us to the ancient town's main bridge. Houses, restaurants, shops—all perched along the riverbanks. As soon as we got off the rickshaw, three elderly women accosted us. Each talking over the top of the other, they held out plastic bags bulging with flickering goldfish.

"What do they want? What are they saying?"

"They're saying you ought to set the fish free."

"To set them free?"

"To buy them and throw them back in the water."

Thrusting a fistful of bills into their hands, I grabbed the bags. I stalked past them, and craning my neck to watch them as they fell, poured the fish into the river.

My husband was waiting for me at the foot of the bridge. He was scanning the water's depths, surrounded by strolling locals and tourists snapping pictures.

"I couldn't stand to see them like that."

He shuffled over to made room for me beside Him. Creaky wooden boats packed with tourists drifted under the bridge. "I suppose it was to be expected," He said after a while.

"Why take that tone of voice? You think what I did was silly?"

He looked at me, pensively. "You know they'll fish them out again, don't you? They'll end up back in the plastic bags. And then a soft-hearted woman like you—"

"A soft-hearted woman? What I did wasn't from soft-heartedness."

"Then from what?"

"I know the value of a life lived to the full, because . . ."

"Because it's what I have denied you. And it feels urgent. Full of mystery."

"Don't mock me."

Silence fell between us again. Abruptly, He said: "I'm not mocking you. How could I mock you? It's just that I would never want you to feel like a fish in a bag. If you felt that way . . ."

"Yes?"

"I would be very sorry."

"And how did You come to the conclusion that I might feel like a fish in a bag?"

"I've been noticing changes."

"Such as?"

"When you speak, you do so hastily and with anger in your voice. And simple things that no one else would notice or deem important bring out a rueful astonishment in you."

"It has been so long since—"

Two girls interrupted me midsentence. Heads gracefully tilted, they asked if we would take their picture. Eagerly, God complied. The girls posed in front of the bridge, making victory signs. Perhaps I ought to have told Him that His secrecy, His irony, were too much for me? But then I would have had to mention *Don Quixote*.

The sky darkened. A drizzle began to fall. It was impossible to continue our conversation.

LOW AWNINGS OVERHUNG the lanes winding through the bazaar. We walked beneath them in single file to avoid getting wet; we lingered by stalls selling fans, fruit, rice rolled tightly inside bamboo leaves, sesame bars. I was hungry. God led me to a café on the riverbank. We ordered pickled cucumber, eggplant, tea.

"Why did You bring me here?" I asked.

"To this café?"

"To this part of the world."

He considered a moment, then said, "There's no belief in heroism, no worship of difficulty here. There are no epics. Significantly, one of their philosophers once said, 'I would do better not to speak at all.'"

"Ah, I see, that's why You like it here."

He smiled. "You like it, too, but you simply won't admit it. Do you know that there is no translation for the word 'purpose' in this country? They believe in the natural inclination of things."

"Oh, right, and in that way, they dispense with all toil and effort."

"They accept that humans are at the beck and call of circumstance, not the other way around."

At a neighboring table, people were loudly sucking on crab shells, then spitting them out on the plastic tablecloth.

"You endorse such fatalism? Aristotle says that even in nature there is struggle—I clearly recall the word ἀγών. It was You who gave me the book."

"The problem is that you read philosophy as if it were carved in stone. Some things just are what they are."

"What do you mean?"

"I mean that I chose this place for no particular reason. I thought that a country with a history, rooted in time, would do us good."

"My country has history, too."

God glanced at me with sadness in His eyes. "You wouldn't recognize it."

"Has it changed so much?"

He turned to look at the river strewn with floating garbage—paper, plastic bags.

"It is nothing like the one you knew."

"Fine," I said, "There's no need to get angry."

"Some things are better left alone."

He sipped His tea. On the plate, the uneaten eggplant had congealed.

Nightfall came early. Over the stalls, red lanterns shone through the dark.

"It's so humid here. Look at how frizzy my hair is!"

In God's kingdom, I had forgotten about rain. It was always unchangingly pleasant, with none of nature's ups and downs. Suddenly, I remembered the meaning of autumn. I began describing withered leaves, heavy clouds. Silently, He watched the boats bobbing on the water, otherworldly in the glow of their lanterns.

"How about a boat ride?" He announced.

HE WAVED TO one of the boatmen, who turned and rowed towards us. Under the boat's patched canvas tarp, we sat down opposite each other on wooden benches. In answer to a question from the boatman, my husband pointed vaguely down the river.

Groaning hollowly, the boat glided over the water, the moon following in our languid wake. The glowing windows that lined the riverbanks. The choreography of the waiters behind restaurant windowpanes. All these kindled a longing for the family life now irrevocably lost to me. Then we turned down a narrow canal, passed under a dark bridge. We were not speaking. I had surrendered myself to the rocking, the darkness, the water, which worked together in synergy.

I did not believe that God had no ulterior motive. He had chosen a country of heat and humidity, whose customs were strange to me. A believer in the power of purpose, I now found myself in a place where everything was left to chance. One night I thought to myself: Am I here of my own free will? Would He miss me if I left? Would He drag me back by the hair like a man in love? Or would He give me up forever?

I would never leave Him, of course. I had no idea how to earn my keep, how to travel. I didn't even know how to cross the road without getting run over. I viewed the practicalities of life through the eyes and the experience of a seventeen-year-old. I did not understand the world. Nor did I know how to discriminate between the essential and the non-essential. I wanted the truth, but I was afraid. "Some things are better left alone."

And why would I leave anyway? Life at His side was endlessly interesting, pleasantly manifold. In the mornings, we visited markets, museums, Buddhist and Taoist temples. We even wandered into a Christian church, all lit up with multicolored lamps like a circus. In the evenings, He took me to dives sizzling with greasy pans and abuzz with listless flies. I ordered everything on the menu, clinking my glass with the other customers'. One night, when I was in the mood for a romantic setting, He took me to a palace on the banks of the lake. I had sweet and sour beef with pancakes. He had greens. As usual, His mind appeared to be elsewhere.

Under one pretext or another, He was always heading to the international bookstore, to visit the fiction section. One day, I decided enough was enough. I pushed the door open and walked into the bookstore. Past the erasers, the notebooks, the sharp pencils—straight to the fiction. As soon as I spied Him stooped over the books, my heart felt like it was going to burst.

"ARE YOU ASLEEP?"

I jolt upright. "No, no." But actually I had fallen asleep with the Bible on my chest, my notes pressed between its pages.

"May I lie down next to you?"

"You don't need to ask."

I roll over on one side, careful not to reveal my pencil. "Sorry to be sleeping in the middle of the bed. I never know if You'll come and how to . . ."

"What are you reading?" He asks without turning to look at me, as if addressing the pillow. As if I don't exist.

"Psalms. 'Turn us, O God of our salvation, and cause thine anger toward us to cease.'"

"I hope you don't mean that literally."

"I don't know. How would I know if You were angry with me? I am still waiting for us to talk."

"About what?"

"Don't pretend You don't know." Fully awake now, I stretch out on my back. I gaze into His eyes.

"Don't get so worked up. And never ask."

"Why?"

"Because time does not exist."

"Now you are just being mean."

"No, I am being utterly objective"

Turning His back to me, He falls asleep instantly. My eyes trace the dark mass of His body, the familiar line of shoulders, back, pelvis. I get up and tiptoe around the bed. Palms braced against my knees, I lean over and stare at Him as if He were an exhibit in a museum. Tangled beard, white mane. He opens large, gleaming eyes. For an interminable moment, we stare at each other.

"I am tired."

"I know. But . . ."

His eyes close again. Immediately His spirit calms (what I like to call His spirit).

I am about to talk about fiction and in front of me lies the greatest fictional character known to humanity. The male body He dons is so convincing, I occasionally forget who He is. It is terrible to think about: the primordial mind trapped within that illusory head, which I'm occasionally allowed to touch. How can I fault Him for His silence when I know that it is part of the meaning of divinity? I imagine Him all alone on the brink of chaos and the balm of forgiveness washes over me, the desire to love Him for what He is. I let Him sleep and head next door to the laundry room. I'm no longer drowsy. I must finish telling you my story.

When we left off, I was entering the bookstore to confront my husband. At the sight of Him stooping over the book display, my heart, you'll recall, felt as if it was going to break. It's odd to catch God doing something forbidden. I knew that each step I took toward Him brought me closer to a painful truth.

"Why are you reading *Don Quixote*?"

"How do you know it is *Don Quixote*?"

"I can see the cover. I know."

"Have you read it?"

"No, but I've heard about it. Are You going to tell me what You're doing here?"

He closed the book and sank into the only armchair. "You've been watching me?"

I knelt at His feet. "Please tell me."

"No." He snapped.

I said that I was weary of the same old story: every day, He made a beeline for the bookstore, only to return to the hotel and fob me off with lies.

"It's been ages since I read a novel," He said. "I shouldn't have picked one up again."

"Shouldn't You? I don't understand."

"There's nothing to understand. Imagination leads us nowhere. Only toward further flights of imagination. Toward inevitable failure."

"I don't believe You."

He looked at me, His face blank, expressionless.

"You're hiding something from me."

His face remained blank.

"You're right," He replied finally. "But there's no other solution. I am beholden."

"To whom?"

"To Myself."

"Are You trying to drive me crazy? You want me to let go of everything and believe in You. But what am I to believe in? Your lies?"

My husband bowed His head without a word.

"I beg you, Lord, I beseech you. Say something. Anything."

No reply. He hasn't talked to me since.

EVERY MORNING, HE left for the bookstore and returned to our room laden with books. I have no idea how He carried them all. Voltaire, Rousseau, Tolstoy, Dickens. Dostoevsky, Musil, Kafka, Schnitzler. Mainly men. Occasionally, a woman: Jane Austen, Virginia Woolf, Katherine Mansfield, Clarisse Lispector. Poetry: Goethe, Milton, Akhmatova. He read desperately, voraciously, as if chasing something always just beyond His reach. Every so often, He would roll over to the other side of the bed. He would sit up, then lie back down again. Day after day, towers of books stacked up higher and higher, covering the walls of the vestibule. He was continually plucking books from stacks, taking great pains to avoid demolishing the entire paper tower. He built stack after stack, one beside the other. Once the vestibule was packed to the rafters, He started piling books in our bedroom.

He no longer went out with me to eat. We stopped going for walks together. Alone, I wandered the neighborhood around the hotel. Taking the subway or bus was out of the question. I would have been lost without my husband. I was constantly looking behind me, fearful that I was being followed, that someone with a hammer or a knife was hot on my heels. For lunch, I'd have a quick bite on a park bench. I would take my food out of its wrapping and chew quickly, stealing stealthy glances at the children and old folks. Hidden threats and dangers lurked everywhere. If someone happened to approach my bench, I got up and beat a hasty retreat.

Shut up in our hotel room, He read all day. He would open the window to stare outside at the road, completely engrossed in His thoughts. If I reached out to stroke His hair, He drew back. When I woke up in the middle of the night, He was invariably sitting in the armchair, reading under the glow of the table lamp.

It was the same here as in His Study: He read a number of books simultaneously, as if they formed a single, larger narrative. He would turn from one book to another, creating small avalanches as He pulled them from their stacks. Tomes tumbled with loud thuds. Together, we stacked them up again. All that time, he said not a word to me. Nothing but nods and gestures.

He no longer turned ghostly at night. He slept beside me like any other weary man—He had even developed the bald patch typical of prolonged bed-rest. This new humanity, combined with His reading mania, unnerved me: was God at risk of an intellectual embolism, a thrombosis of the spirit? I knew how much He loved reading, but this wasn't love; it was an obsession.

The need to protect Him stirred within me. I can hear you laugh: me? protect God? But please remember that He was everything to me: husband, teacher, father, mother, house, heartless brother. I cannot describe exactly how it happened, what were the silent stirrings of the heart that kindled my blind devotion once again. The love I felt for Him was like the love from our time in the Forest. And love, despite what He says about the natural inclination of things, lends purpose.

You sense selfishness in what I'm saying? You wonder whether my devotion to my husband was ultimately self-serving, a safe haven in a world that struck me as frightening and strange? As God is my witness, it never occurred to me. The only obstacle to our relationship continued to be His aloofness, as well as something related to our circumstances: a certain sense of finitude. The feelings I harbored for Him had no place in time. You need a lifetime to be able truly to understand someone. You need an eternity to understand God.

"MAY I READ one of these books, too?" I asked one day. Having washed our clothes and hung them up to dry in the bathroom. Having ordered out for food. Having looked out the window untold times.

Silently, He handed me a stack of novels in translation. I started with *A Man Without Qualities* by Robert Musil. The protagonist, Ulrich, is stifled by the human qualities that define his lot, or at least that's how I interpreted his situation. Musil believes that during an era in our distant past, poetry and prosaic everyday experience were one and the same. That's when life had meaning.

My mind dwelt on that primordial era of meaning, as if it were something I remembered, something I had lived. As if I had written the book I was reading: each sentence illumined, but at the same time obscured what I already knew. A game of hide-and-seek with words and meaning, punctuated by sudden quivering flashes of insight. Each time I had a thought that seemed to remind me of something, another arrived like a crashing wave to wash away the fleeting memory. Paradoxically, I found myself both closer to and farther from understanding. Imagine trying to get up from your chair and falling flat on your face, even though you clearly remember what it is to walk. That's what it felt like.

Why did Musil talk about life's hidden meaning instead of

revealing it to me? Why was he standing in front of the window
that let in the light required to dissipate the mysteries of darkness? Why was he obstructing the very view he was describing? It
infuriated me. Grasping the book, I flung it into a corner of the
room. My husband looked up from the volume He was reading
(*The Red and the Black* by Stendhal, I think it was).

"Exactly," He said, after a pause. "That's exactly what I would
like to do, too."

I began reading because I wanted to understand what was
happening to Him. It had not occurred to me that reading would
unnerve me, too, to such an extent; would plunge me into such
utter disorientation. How to explain in words the entanglements
of the heart, the abandoned country within, which I discovered
as I read? Yes, there I was, reading about everything I had denied
myself, watching it rise before me, alive and pulsing in all its
vibrant glory. God and I lay next to each other, turning the pages
as we, too, turned from side to side. Occasionally, we wept—His
tears were silent, dignified, quickly wiped away with the back of
His hand; mine came in tremulous bursts that clouded my mind,
the same as back in the day with Auntie.

Eager not to waste time, I ate in bed. I always dropped the
plastic bag of leftovers in the corridor and then opened the window to air the room. When He ventured out for supplies, I
followed behind, dragging my feet. Within weeks (or perhaps it
was months), I had forgotten how to walk. The sight of people
reminded me of the television in our room: all noise, no plot.
Laden with books we'd climb into a taxi and head straight to our
hotel. We ascended to the third floor, bathed in the dim light
of the elevator.

Every morning, the housekeepers tried to evict us from the
room. At first, they knocked on the door. Later, once they had
gotten used to us, they entered uninvited. As the water flowed
in the bathroom, we focused on getting to the end of our pages.
Then, holding our books (His: Gombrowicz, Maupassant, Keats;
mine: Calvino, Chekov, Goethe), we would stand in the corridor
until they finished cleaning. Day by day, the number of volumes
grew. There was no longer any space for the housekeepers.

Walls of books towered around us. A mere sliver of a path
led from the bed to the door. We informed reception that we no
longer needed room service. Now at liberty to do as we pleased,
we stacked books under the bed. In our small wardrobe. In the
bathroom. First, in the bidet, then in the large, deep bathtub. I
washed in the sink, careful not to drip anywhere.

A deepening of the darkness outside our third-floor window,
as the cars honked on the street below, heralded the arrival of
winter. I did not open the window to catch snowflakes in my
hands. I had no interest in that type of sensation.

My body ached from immobility. Beneath my skull, my mind
bubbled and boiled, singing a version of the Ode to Joy. Instead
of echoing Schiller, "World, can you sense your Creator?" I sang,
"Creator, can you sense your World." On His side of the bed,
He smiled conspiratorially, as if guessing my thoughts. Tired and
happy, I would bury my book under my pillow and succumb to
dreamless sleep.

How to talk about literature? I draw you a picture instead.
Some people find no pleasure in a mechanically inclining bed
because it reminds them that one day they will grow old and
die. Such people are called writers. They imagine a drama and
strive to find the words with which to turn it into narrative. The
worst amongst them are the poets: like drunks they lurch and
totter from syllable to syllable, from consonant to vowel, from
diphthong to triphthong, only to fall, dragging down everything
with them. Often, even meaning itself.

What I *can* talk about is the anger I felt as I read; about anger
evolving into understanding; about understanding evolving into
habit. But first, I must ask you a question: in Musil's book, who do
you think is standing in front of the window, blocking the view?
Don't you see? It's God. A God without qualities lent me a book
about a man without qualities. What remained with me from
Musil, was this: "God does not mean the world literally. It is a
metaphor, an analogy, a figure of speech to which He has to resort
for some reason or other, and it never satisfies Him, of course. We
are not supposed to take Him at His word, it is we ourselves who
must come up with the answer to the riddle He sets us."

And that is what I did. I found my own answers—a vague self-reliance—in fiction. What I hadn't learned while I was still living in the world, I picked up from reading novels. Together with the protagonists, I experienced the requisite rites of passage: finding a job, getting fired, experimenting with drugs, drowning. I learned how to do a sexy strip-tease; how to play the piano, chess, poker; how to raise my glass to make a toast at a reception; how to work in aristocratic kitchens; how to break rocks in coal mines. I learned how to give birth and raise children; how to marry them off and then lose them in an industrial accident. I learned how to perform open-heart surgery, to conquer villages with my cavalry, to exact revenge, to use my fists, to stab, to serve prison sentences, to grow old. As I lay beside the protagonist in his grave, rotting next to his bones, I even learned how to die. At first, I seethed with anger at the places I had not visited, at the idylls I had not lived. Later, I even yearned for all that was evil and destructive: dastardly plots, murders, wars. Within me stirred curiosity, a fervent interest in humans and their blind drive to throw caution to the winds as they struggle toward death, towards re-birth.

Writers taught me how to live with everything I could not endure. In theological texts, in philosophy, I found either revealing analogies and methodical explanations, or generalities and evasions. Even mystical texts arrived at studiously prepared conclusions. In fiction, however, it was no holds barred. Animals talk; fathers turn into crabs, sons into beetles; the world comes to an end; and people are as indifferent to time as if they were gods. Actions are heroic, misguided, unprecedented, yet always somehow accurate. Unsolvable riddles. Loose ends. Life, that bonfire of the vanities, becomes a rehearsal for something nobler, simpler, more forgiving that I could not yet grasp. As for my husband, I bumped into Him everywhere. "I am jealous of everything whose beauty does not die," I read in the *Portrait of Dorian Grey*. "No God! We have had too much God! Away with God!" exclaims James Joyce. "Alas, I was alone, alone on this earth," sighs Chateaubriand.

That's how I got hooked. Gradually, I stopped seeing both

Him and myself in the fictional protagonists I encountered. I opened myself up to meeting other beings in all their strangeness, villainy, or charm. Later, I found something more elusive still, something that escaped me as I reached to grasp it in my hand, something that went deep. By then, everything I read, I read as allegory, as possibility. What was happening to me was what Schopenhauer describes: "It is the same in literature as in life. Wherever one goes one immediately comes upon the incorrigible mob of humanity. It exists everywhere in legions, crowding, soiling everything, like flies in summer." In the foregoing quotation, what probably struck you was the image of the flies. What struck me was the analogy between life and fiction. I take it one step further: in fiction, the sky shines brighter; characters are truer to their inclinations; food tastes better; and as for love—it pierces the heart. It is as if life is whispering to you: this is what I would be, if I took myself seriously.

That was how I lived. I lived amidst the tumult of simulated life, in a constant upheaval of the imagination, a frenzy of interpretation. A man reads tales of chivalry and begins to believe he is a knight. Another, locks himself in the office, muttering, "I would prefer not to." A third hunts a white whale. And the women? One hurls herself onto the railroad tracks; another, suffocating in provincial ennui, takes a lover; a third agonizingly makes her way to the lighthouse. Yes, women in fiction are the same as women in life. They marry the wrong men; they have a boatload of children; they die of consumption, or stick their head in an oven to roast their brains.

Remember what He said? "Imagination takes us nowhere. Only to further flights of imagination. To inevitable failure." I see us locked in that suffocating room, watching the chronicle of that failure. Gasping and gagging on the poisonous fumes of fiction, I kept taking deep breaths and turning the pages. Just a moment—why did I do that? To come to grips with the life I hadn't lived? To keep my husband company? Was it pure masochism on my part? Or was it a premonition of the terrible knowledge that now loomed for me?

Who has first dibs on imagination? Who is the greatest

dream-weaver of all? Who wrote fiction before fiction? Don't delay, I beg you. Hurry, hurry! Meet me in the place where everything I say makes sense. That's where I will wait for you, to tell you everything I learned and console you as best I can.

I'm not sure if I'll find a better time to tell you: You are a saint of a person. If you did not exist, I would invent you.

PARADISO

Forgive, O Lord, my little jokes on Thee,
and I'll forgive Thy great big one on me.

Robert Frost

A DARKNESS AS deep as God's inertia. Statically, He cogitated, without images, without words. All He knew was darkness and solitude. He wanted nothing more, for He did not know how to want.

It all began when a yellow flare tore through the benighted chaos. What was it? Where did it come from? We will never know how that beginning came to be: whether it was God or chaos itself, for God and chaos are one. In the wake of that first flare, He invented a yellow lamp and hung it in the darkness. Now that He could see, He invented dramatic bursts: volcanic eruptions, lightning bolts, meteorites blazed through the night. Hankering for a longer-lasting light, He made the sun. If He'd known how to weep, He would have shed tears of joy for its fiery brilliance. But all that darkness had turned Him inward. He created clouds to externalize His brooding.

In the beginning, the clouds were lowering silhouettes in the heavens, two-dimensional dark blue stains. Then, they turned into pitted pumice stones. Still, God was not satisfied with the clouds. He experimented with their characteristics, their density until they looked like condensed smoke. The Second Coming transformed them once and for all into repositories of rain. (Yes, the Second Coming has come and gone. We like to think it is still in the future because we fear the end of the world. All our metaphysical claims derive from this fear.)

As a counterpoint to the weightiness of His thoughts, He created a yellow butterfly. The butterfly took wing, but God did not bat an eye. Returning to the ethereal symmetry of its blueprint, He forged thousands, millions of butterflies. They scattered far and wide. Nostalgic for the velvet surface of their wings, He created leaves and hung them on trees; new shoots sprouted radiant among the branches. He tried to raise the trunks upright, but each time they fell with a booming clatter. They needed firm ground for their roots. So He invented the earth. In the beginning, it was bright yellow, like the wings of the first butterfly. After His initial enthusiasm wore off, He replaced it with a neutral color not so jarring to the eye.

Next came the wind. Its soft sighs made the leaves of the trees tremble and dance like butterfly wings. Its violent gusts scattered them like whirling confetti over the earth. To tame the winds, He created mountains, set them in towering rectangular fences. They were a disappointing sight. He forged waterways and rivers, cleaving rock, sculpting mountains into rounded peaks. He liked water. Out of curiosity, He splashed it all around, and thus the seas came into being. He invented dolphins for the water, and ushered them into roaming herds. Their synchronous dives, their shrill cries amused Him.

He gave His creations names, endowed them with voice. Fascinated by contradiction, He made birds roar and mammoths whistle. Animals now roamed freely over the globe, but He yearned for something still and delicate, something akin to His own consciousness. This led to the most phantasmagoric of His handiwork: flowers, petals, sepals, and, buried deep inside the pistil's gourd, concealed ovaries. (They were named ovaries only later, when everything had to have purpose).

Beset by qualms that life was becoming too soft and easy, He summoned a tiger to disembowel a deer. Or He invented something sour, like a lemon. Something impregnable, like a turtle-shell. His fascination with the microscopic led to amoebas and bacteria. His interest in the mechanics of erosion and penetration led to gorges and the primary sexual organs. When He encountered pitfalls in His ontology, He changed tactics. Did the whale's clumsy, splashing dive contradict His vision of stately stillness? Lo and behold, He created barren, whale-shaped islands. In those primordial times, my abstracted husband was drawn from invention to invention by a process of association. From butterfly to leaf, from leaf to tree, from tree to soil.

It was all a big game to Him: the arched neck of the camel, chicken, pigeon. Snail shells. Penguins and seahorses. Cacti, pomegranate seeds, the cuckoo pint's poker-shaped hood. He was able to improve on His creations as He pleased, but He could not retract them. The unwritten law by which He abided was unbridled beauty, aesthetic vitality. The kangaroo, the flamingo, the antelope of the savanna were all testaments to His flights of fancy. The purple frogs of India, the peacock. The pacu fish with its human teeth. The fossil-like goblin shark of the ancient *Mitsukurinidae* genus. Homo sapiens.

Humans came late to the world. For some time, God had been dreaming of a strong yet resilient being, smooth and soft of skin yet deep and dark of soul. He kept having second thoughts, he kept going back to the drawing board, over and over again: skeleton, ears, the web of blood and brain, the breadth of throat. By planting humans on their feet, He freed their arms. In an unprecedented flash of inspiration, He created the center of speech. He worked on perfecting tongue, vocal chords, palate.

When the beings He had invented began freely roaming the newly-built earth, Creation slipped from His grasp. The result was alliances, enmities, conflagrations. Insects assailed plants, rabbits trembled in fear, bats hung upside down. When God invented snow, even He was awed by the incomparable sight. Scattering it all around to see what would happen, fruit froze on trees, sodden earth slid down hillsides. Seeking warmth, humans skinned animals. Fleeing beasts huddled in caves.

He sensed that the period of pure aesthetic pleasure, of play for its own sake, was coming to an end. The life He had created was begging Him to desist from the joys of further invention, to focus on taming the extremes of climate instead. He had to solve the problem of sustenance, to provide His creatures with comfort, with shelter. It shook Him. How, purposefully and unerringly, to strike a balance between living organisms and their environment? How to think through the macroeconomics of it all? What should bloom where? Who should feed on whom? And what, He wondered, did a life not based on pure consciousness hold in store for the future of creation? The blithesome flight of the butterflies was a thing of the past. To answer these questions, He had to invent a compelling narrative arc for that first butterfly. How it emerged from its cocoon (it had to have come from somewhere); how it fluttered from flower to flower (for food); how it folded its wings to die.

He had to gather His wits. His casual experiment, a spontaneous plunge into the abyss, had failed. Scurrying into the first cave He encountered, He curled up in its depths. If He had had a heart, He would have driven a stalactite through it. But immortality deals a fatal blow to action. God did not flee to the darkness to ponder His fate. His only desire was to stop hurting. He therefore invented sleep.

He awoke to a terrifying world. Bloated corpses of His own making bobbed on cataclysmic floods. The sun, His brightest achievement, had turned into a turgid crimson giant. The sense of defeat that had driven Him to seek shelter in the cave was replaced by an unprecedented urgency. He rolled up His sleeves and began the job of cleaning up. Oh, the self-sacrifice it took to wander the earth, sealing the chasms left by earthquakes, burying human and animal!

Inconsolable, yet ferociously determined, He revisited Creation with renewed vigor. He turned to the sun again, this time bent on composing a more convincing story of brightness. He mixed hydrogen with sunlight; experimented with magnetic fields and the density of natural gases; was discouraged by shockwaves, nuclear fusion, the first pale photons. Finally, He designed an exemplary structure: around a flaming core, He built a layered sphere. It was His way of endowing creation with meaning and unity. Within each being, at the heart of every interrelation, He instilled fear and a set of natural inclinations, along with a dash of His own nostalgia for a now lost, completely whimsical perfection. This was His Second Coming.

Perched on the peaks of the tallest mountain, He began His calculations. He filled scroll upon scroll with equations and diagrams. The same question, over and over again: how to design a convincing evolutionary narrative. He examined everything He'd done up to that point. Did roaring birds make sense? No, He decided, and invented birdsong instead. He reserved roaring for the larger creatures that sprang from His fervid imagination one by one: elephants, tigers, lions. He revisited His previously desultory compositions and designed detailed generative organs for both flora and fauna. He invented a vast assortment of fructiferous trees. To cover His tracks, He concealed fossils of the ancient plant *Archaefructus liaoningensis* in a cave, and buried a partial skeleton of the alleged *Homo sapiens idaltu* in an Ethiopian river bed. In the dying embers of the Second Coming He concealed yet another red herring. Human progress, the future invention of the telescope, were sure to lead to the discovery of primordial gravitational waves and thereby the structure of His invented universe. He aimed to mislead future researchers with layers of fake history, with smoke screens that would allow human beings to endure their lives.

Why cover His tracks? Because the evolution from play to deception had taken Him to a higher sphere of truth, both abstract and tragic. And to extreme disquiet. Oh, how He wished to leave it all behind! To build Himself a refuge of trees, lakes, forests where He might hide, forget, and be forgotten. Yes, He longed for shelter, for the plush, immortal embrace of the natural world He had conjured in the darkness.

Once it was completed, He was assailed by loneliness. Habituated by now to interaction, involvement, He did not know what to do with Himself. So He began reading. In books, He became reacquainted with humanity. He reveled in their passions, their inner identification with Him. Soon, however, myths, ideas, equations, were not enough. So He started getting married, choosing women or men with a flair for existential angst. That was the way He liked them: inconsolable, open-hearted. When the time was ripe, He plucked them—firmly, determinately— from the world. Yes, just like He did me. He was not absolute in His proclivities. Nor did one relationship substitute for another. Once, He married a dove. Another time, the final mammoth. After death, His companions became Angels. They formed a community, taking care of His new partner until death added another disciple to their holy order.

That was His version, simplified and retold as fairytale. Now, here is my version.

Once upon a time, God, all alone, was talking to Himself. "Once upon a time" means something you and I cannot comprehend. In God's language there are multitudes of untranslatable words, feelings, ideas. Even He cannot find the words to describe what existed before the world came to be; the assault against chaos; the passage from idea to tangible reality. This task, in human terms, was best undertaken by theologians and philosophers. But they were successful only up to a point.

Spinoza addressed the mind and extension of God. He did not comment on other predicates of the divine presence. Pascal describes it thus: "an immensity of spaces whereof I know nothing, and which know nothing of me." The act of interpretation finds consonance in God. That is how He too thinks when He tries to mimic our powers of perception. Yet the converse is also true: He does not understand our language. The meaning of entropy (which He so beautifully elaborated on when I told Him about the rotten apple with my mother's teethmarks) is beyond God. This is not surprising. You do not fear a thing that poses no threat to you. His lack of fear and understanding do not lessen His love. You want proof? The Second Coming.

All creators love their creations, but His love, because it anticipated all others, is fundamentally, exponentially more powerful. When Lacan said that to love is to give what you do not have, because only by accepting your lack are you able to love, he came close to God's way of speaking about this feeling. Can you hear the tragic pulse of unfulfillment in this sentence?

Many would like to believe that God's plan stumbled up against human repudiation. A convenient excuse for beings like us, who feed on guilt. In reality, the plan stumbled up against God's own inability to create a world worthy of Him. Not ethically, but rather intellectually, sensually. A world that might discourse with God on an equal basis.

The Fall pertains to Creation itself, not to humanity.

OH, I KNOW so many things! Yes, I'm bragging, succumbing to the sin of *superbia*. How to curb my enthusiasm for discovery? Light as a butterfly wing, I sit in my chair in the laundry room and lunge relentlessly forward, in conceptual leaps and bounds. In my youth, such leaps and bounds were literal, over the cryogenic expanses of a sunless, moonless world.

I am not trying to ape fiction writers. They describe things that never existed as if they actually did. I am speaking about something that actually exists as if it never had. The success of this endeavor is not mine. It is the result of the absence of time in God's kingdom. Of the prevailing sense of discontinuity.

Have I described my pencil yet? It's a 2B, soft and dark. Peeling because of its moist hiding place. Every morning, I pull on the string and out it comes, warm as a human finger. I sharpen it frugally—it's the only one I have—using our very best knife. I must also tell you about the paper. It's made out of rags. Soaked, pulped, and wrung out to dry.

Ah, you think I'm rambling? I know, you want to know how God conceived of matter before the invention of matter, light before the invention of light. How did He tell History before History? Was He in a hurry or did He linger over the details (birds' beaks, human buttocks, sunsets)? Did He learn from us or can He not stand the sight of us?

"Uncertain is the will of God." Never fear—I'm teasing.

IF HUMANS HAD God's vocabulary at their disposal, they would not require the word "faith" in order to compensate for all that is inarticulable, for naked thought. When we first met, when I first opened my eyes and saw Him sitting beside me on the bed, He spoke to me of faith. Remember? He knew that I would not understand all that which (if He were being merciful and kind) He needed to warn me about. Yes, I know, He educated me. Yet He was well aware that human nature ends where God's begins. God had eyes that could see far and wide and deep. And He was stuck explaining the world to a blind woman.

Religious pseudohistory cannot be blamed for the wide range

of its interpretations of divinity: from the ancient belief in the divinity of the soul and the faceless gods of the Stoics to the gods who demanded that both the Aztecs and Abraham sacrifice their children. These flights of fancy are, after all, the tools for constructing such histories, their driving force. But what about Him? Why did He not create a world to our measure? Why did He plant human beings inside history like decorative puppets dotting the landscape: inside caves, clinging to the base of mountains, corralled in the first cities? In our first version, we were completely primal beings, genuine apes. We endured the tempestuous fear of night through sheer strength of feeling, not through reason. We then evolved into what we are today: selfish and grasping, primal at heart, but girded with the armor of culture. We evolved teleologically, in ways that He had foreseen, but could not forestall. It is wrong to believe that the meaning of Creation is evident in God's interventions. Creation has no meaning beyond itself. Ultimately, He remained true to the childish egotism of His nature. Despite the mirage of progress He conjured up to deceive us, His primary interest was always His own entertainment.

Why not call things by their proper name? The Great Teacher, it turns out, is powerless to deflect death, to bar our return to the chaotic darkness. Except that He isn't really a Teacher. He is the primordial Author. In the beginning, He built the world with the word. The second time around, making use of scrolls and notes. Erect and composed in the midst of all that chaos, like Vladimir Nabokov.

You say it is blasphemy to compare God to a self-exiled author who liked to write standing up while contemplating the lake opposite his hotel window? Very well, let's examine the image together: God abandons His true state of being in order to go into voluntary exile and, in one fell swoop, He creates the world. He is bewitched by the softness of snow, the human ear, horses' haunches . The artist within Him rejoices at the setting sun, the sculptor, at knees and joints. Then, after He makes a mess of things, He flees from the consequences into the oblivion of hibernation. When He awakes, He mops up the blood, and designs it all anew, starts from scratch. He stands there helplessly, at the window, gazing out over the unruffled waters of the lake, watching as His creatures strive and struggle. He needs us as much as we need Him, but He will never admit it. He remained firm in His resolution never to betray Creation, never to cage it or turn it into a laboratory of controlled experiments, a conveyor belt of salvation, with machines purring night and day as they manufacture happiness. Utilitarianism, too, has its limits.

When He spoke to me of this paradox, my husband was referencing the meaning of Aristotelian impotence. When you know the right thing to do but hesitate to act. Indeed, what else could He do? It was always already too late for the world. Overcome by guilt, He'd decide to intervene (I am not sure what exactly corresponds to "guilt" and "intervention" in His vocabulary), but His miracles always ended up attesting to His compromised position. They smacked of the contrived conclusions to trashy novels. Novels barely deserving of the name, not worth the paper they are printed on. God never once brought this kind of novel into our room.

As for His own Book—with its transcendentalism, cosmic perspective, the devastating postmodernism of its Original Concept—it is the most radical, the most earthshaking work of all time. Do you know why? Because it contained the first idea—the idea behind all other ideas—and the first failure. As Voltaire said in the wake of the Lisbon earthquake that devoured a hundred thousand devout souls praying in their churches: both the faithful and the faithless expired at the capricious hand of the natural laws that came into being when the world was created. And there was God, the ultimate dispassionate observer. Must I repeat the word? Entropy.

He admitted that He was powerless to save me if I fell from the window, now that the fabled homogenization of matter had been set in motion. Despite the fact that He is one with Nature, my husband cannot lock horns with her. He deems it unethical.

Phew, I gave vent to all that without even pausing for breath! It was the only way. The time has come to talk about the particulars of our trip. You are tired of trying to keep up, and I am tired of putting it off.

I want you to know that these pages have been an ordeal for me. Pure torment. I wish I could use God's words, but how? What I write is mere approximation, nothing but a trace of the truth. Not because I'm lying, but because I am translating His thoughts into human ones. I am like those bad translators who capture the main idea, but betray the harmony of the form and content. I had hoped to compose this letter by stitching together fragments of essays by authors wiser than me. But where would I find their work? We left it all behind when God decided that it was time to give up writing and go back to our timeless world.

Would you like to know how He came clean? He reached into the pocket of His shirt, pulled out a sheet of paper, unfolded it, and then in His soft, weary voice began to read the words of Nietzsche: "I know my fate." He glanced at me to make sure I was paying attention and continued: "One day my name will be associated with the memory of something tremendous—a crisis without equal on earth, the most profound collision of conscience."

Now, you are probably asking yourself how my reticent husband, whom I'd practically lost to the siren call of books, came to talk about the creation of the world. One reason was that I abandoned Him. Yes, you read that correctly: I abandoned Him. My disappearance prompted His desire for revelation, at least that is what I believe. Don't forget that we were living somewhere foreign to Him. His judgement was already somewhat impaired, and fiction had only compounded His disorientation.

It was an echo of the past, of what had occurred centuries before my birth when He pored over Babylonian versions of the Gilgamesh (sadly not preserved for the rest of us), over the Mahabharata, over Homeric epics, ancient tragedies, the poetry of Sappho. Yes, exactly the same thing had happened when He pored over Sanskrit hymns to the two brothers who climb the Himalayas and fall to their deaths (oh, mountains!), over the epic adventures of a sea-tossed warrior fending off Cyclops, Sirens, and suitors on his arduous way home. This is what happened: He felt a terrible sense of threat. He did not comprehend the meaning of homeland, family, power. He, the greatest power, could not conceive of the agony of separation, doubt, death. (What did "marriage bed" mean to God, I wonder? Or "brotherly love," "demigod," "armor," "born a slave") He resolved to banish fiction from His as-yet-unbuilt kingdom. Fiction as a practice of human freedom would remind Him eternally, or at least for the duration of the world's existence, of His own failure.

You are probably wondering why He focused on fiction and not philosophical or theological texts. I've told you what fiction means to me, but I have not yet fully described its effects on Him. It made Him suffer from an ontological vertigo. He would grasp His head in His hands and stumble around the room propping Himself up against the wall. He would open the window and stare up at the sky like a soul in despair.

Philosophy is the practice of making hypotheses. Fiction takes a wild guess and leaps recklessly into the void. Naturally, sometimes it lands on life, sometimes on death, and in both the one case and the other, it soars and plummets with a devilish cackle. The cackling in our hotel room made God frantic. In breaks between reading, His face softened. In novels, life had greater reality, perceptions were sharper. Fictional characters were closer to an original conception of beauty, complexity, the light of the first sun. Sooner or later, He would get angry: yet again, He had been led astray by a lie, a fabrication, a mind-numbing drug. Yet again, here was the echo of that terrible Second Coming.

On our way to the bookstore, He would cast me a pointed glance and fall silent. I learned to recognize that look. As strangers brushed past us, my husband and I penetrated the marrow of existence.

Creation has no meaning beyond itself.

WHAT IS IT I'm doing? Trying to be clever? What is this nonsense I'm babbling? It's not as if I invented the wheel. You ought to have seen me last night, how tormented I was. One moment, I was sitting at the table in the laundry room, the next I had toppled my chair. I upended the table along with all its papers, bolted down the stairs two by two, and sprinted to the Forest. I was drowning.

I flung myself to the ground, by the roots of the plane tree, and began pummeling the trunk as if it were to blame, as if it were my husband. My knuckles became raw and bloody. My shrieks shook the tall grasses and wildflowers. Oh, I was a lion ravening to disembowel the world! Digging deep in the earth, I ripped up God's beautiful greenery in frantic clumps. But immediately it bloomed again. As I've already told you, there are no cracks, no imperfections in our zombie Forest.

Faster and faster, I pulled up those roots. I wanted to outstrip that strange world's uncanny speed of regeneration. But I couldn't. With broken, soil-caked nails, weeping bitter tears, I collapsed on the unearthly earth. I was convinced that everything had come to an end, that I would die there, by the roots of that tree. But somehow the Angels found me, and I awoke in our bed. Which is where I am writing now, chest heavy, throat still sore, as if I had swallowed nettles. My nails, however, are as clean as clean can be! I picture them gathered around me, scrubbing and scrubbing with their nailbrushes. *Fchhhht, Fchhhhht.*

As soon as I opened my eyes, I worried they might have found my papers and pencil. Fortunately, everything was where I had left it. I now write to you in bed, the Bible draped over my knees. I asked the Angels not to disturb me. I want—I need—to talk to you about the rest of our journey.

BOOKS EVERYWHERE, NOW having filled in even the narrow path to our bed. A floor on top of the floor. We would take our shoes off at the threshold and walk barefoot over the stacks. Clambering up peaks and stumbling down stepped tiers. Magic mountains, long valleys of books.

The books that did not fit anywhere else we stuffed under the mattress (*War and Peace, Tristram Shandy, Remembrance of Things Past, The Odyssey, The Old Testament, Dante's Inferno*). We tried to create an even layer of books, a mattress under the mattress. But I would wake in the middle of the night complaining of pain in my sides or neck. "You'll get used to it, little princess," He would answer, with a wink, before returning to His book. Those winks were a new habit of my husband's, acquired after He started reading fiction again.

Every day, He devoured three to four novels and a number of poetry collections. I could not keep up with such a storming pace. Not to mention that I often, very humanly, succumbed to emotion. "What's wrong? Why are you crying?" God would ask. And I would describe what had happened to Werther, Juliette, Hans Castorp or Claudia; to Walter Faber, who unwittingly fell in love with his own daughter. It just so happened that the examples I dwelt on often related to affairs of the heart. He did not like that. He could not understand that ill-starred love affairs, separations, are to us mortals a little foretaste of death.

He read things differently. Only God knows how. I think He was mainly concerned with how certain actions acquire a veneer of heroism. He disliked heroism, ambition, purpose (remember how He talked about the natural inclination of things?). His preferences reflected His conflicted feelings about creation. Imagination terrified Him, but it also stimulated Him with its infinite possibilities and combinations. I remember as clearly as day the fury with which He flung Dante's *Purgatorio* across the room when He read the line, "Then fell within my lofty fantasy one crucified."

"Careful! Someone is going to get hurt!" I warned. He never listened. This flinging became His ritual curse on the book He'd just finished reading. On the other hand, perhaps this was His way of converting the sorrow of separation into fury—a trait typical of my husband's character. I would turn to look at Him. A terrible sight: eyebrows raised, eyes flaming, lips parted, beard quivering under His labored breath. If He were human, I would have diagnosed a raging fever. Is this how divine fever manifests itself? All flashing eyes and flying books?

One day, what I feared came to pass. On my return from the bookstore, I tripped over a low stack in the foyer. As I tottered, my shoulder brushed against a taller stack, which collapsed against another even taller, and it, in turn, against a third. An avalanche of books tumbled down on me. With a sudden jolt, I found myself buried under a heavy mound. I had landed with all my weight on my wrists. On the way to the hospital, they started swelling.

The x-ray revealed that both wrists were broken in the same place. They anesthetized me and joined the bones back together again. When I awoke, my arms were in casts. "Six weeks," the doctor said. God suddenly became interested in the workings of human time.

HE KNOCKS ON the door, enters. I scramble to stuff my papers between the pages of the Bible.

"You were raving in a fever."

"What was I saying?"

"That you had to rip up all the grass, all the trees. And then, that you had to mop."

I laugh nervously. "What else?"

"You said that you had to clean everything until it sparkled."

"What did You make of that?"

"Me?"

"Go on, tell me. You know how much I like Your interpretations."

He sits at the head of the bed in that posture we both know so well. There I am, either wet, depressed, or incapacitated after an accident. And He, as always, seated and impassive, back straight, hands on knees.

"In some languages the root of the verb 'to clean,' means 'to exterminate.' Or 'to wander around without purpose.' But not in your language."

"Let Your good spirit be my guide in the land of righteousness," I tease.

"Is that the only prayer you know?"

"It's the prayer my aunt taught me after my parents' car veered off the road as it was going around a bend."

He paused. "You know how to put me in my place."

"Likewise."

"Will you tell me what you were doing in the Forest?"

"Taking a walk."

"I heard you were hurling yourself at tree trunks."

"Exaggerations. I don't know what to do with all this pent-up energy."

"You have your magnum opus," He says. "The journey continues."

I swallow hard. "What magnum opus?"

"The Bible. What else?"

Our conversations have become pointed, vitriolic, bitter. Scathing, neurotic, ambivalent. After our journey into fiction, it is as if we were writing our own novel.

WHERE WERE WE? Ah, yes, my accident. On our way back from the hospital, God talked about the heavens—a lesson in cosmogony, etymology, and science all rolled into one. Through the cab window, the stars twinkled, bored holes in the wintry surface of sky. It was Confucius, I think, who described them like that: holes through which shines the light of the infinite. It looked fake to me. A yellowed photograph of an expiring universe.

"We should go back," I said.

Startled, He turned to me. "You're tired of it?"

"No," I replied. "I just don't understand how the world works."

"This world."

"Why? Are there others?"

Deep in thought, God contemplated me.

"You must get better first. After that, we'll go back."

"I don't like the world, I never liked it. I don't understand anything."

"You're not the only one."

"It's hard."

"What do you mean?"

"Everyday life is hard. The streets stink and the people don't apologize when they bump into us. They don't see us. They anxiously count their money, as if counting rocks in a labor camp."

"They live in a labor camp."

"Yes, exactly, a labor camp. Why do You let them live like that?"

"I am not responsible for the way they live."

"Only in novels are there people who know how to live. Who actually notice the sun, the color of things. Who actually think."

"Well, they ought to do that in real life as well. It's theirs to live."

"No, no, that statement betrays the privileges of Your position. The entire universe is Your oyster."

"You're in pain and talking nonsense."

"I am in pain. And our bed will only make things worse."

Back in our room, He put me down in an armchair and cleared a path through the books. He put the painkillers on the bedside table. He took the books out from under our mattress. He smoothed the sheets.

I looked at Him with pleading eyes. "Can we leave?"

"Go to sleep. Tomorrow, we'll see."

It was the first time He had used the word "tomorrow." Tomorrow: a word as round and yellow as the moon.

I REACHED OUT; a dense darkness swallowed my arms. My feet were against the headboard, the room upside down.

"God!"

Blindly, I patted the pillows. He moved, but didn't speak. With characteristic lassitude, He rose and opened the shutters. The sky was awash with small, wispy clouds. I clearly remember the blinding light. When I opened my eyes again, I realized that I was in an unfamiliar room full of antique wood furniture: dresser, wardrobe, desk. I sat up in bed, lowering first one leg, then the other to the floor. My feet sank into a rose-patterned rug.

"Careful! Your wrists!"

"Where are we?"

Our balcony hung over a sheer drop. I went to the open door. Below me, as far as my eyes could see, there were sparkling seas, swaying fir trees.

"Don't cry. Calm down."

"Have You brought me . . ."

"No, but we are very close. I didn't want the sound of your mother tongue to upset you. Here, you will heal faster."

I walked onto the black- and white-tiled balcony; filled my lungs with the salty sea breeze. The flames in the distance, between the branches of trees, were the sun.

"Why are you crying? Are you in pain?"

I leaned against His chest. The casts kept me from putting my arms around Him.

"Come now, calm down."

My cheek on His chest, I whispered: "And the Lord, He brought me to His bower."

Like the gazelle, like the wild deer in one of our favorite poems, my husband replied: "Rise up, my love, my fair one, and come away. For, lo, the winter is past; the rain is over and gone. The flowers appear on the earth; the time of the singing of birds is come, and the voice of the turtle dove is heard in our land."

As if springing from the recited verses, a flock of swallows fluttered over the horizon. They hovered for a moment before diving headlong into the unknown.

PERCHED ATOP A covered well, you forget what lurks beneath. The act of lifting the lid naturally coincides with a rediscovery of feeling, with a deepening of love. My husband and I never exchanged glances or secret caresses, like lovers do. Meaningful glances, hungry kisses, gasping mouths: all banished by the idiosyncrasies of our arrangement. My devotion to Him was the other face of submission. I don't know, you tell me: Is what I am describing typical of the way all humans voluntarily yield to those they love?

In the books I read, I often found God, in the form of prayer, hope, utopia. On that promontory by the sea, I discovered my husband. Even though I know He does not like that word, I will use it: it was a miracle. Our love blossomed into something serene and sweet, into a love the likes of which you find not even in novels.

Every morning we got up, breakfasted on our balcony, and went down to stroll by the sea on the Riviera. When we felt like it, we'd rest on one of the benches along the paved promenade. It was spring. Wildflowers poked through the asphalt. Houses with decorated facades similar to ours studded the rocky mountainsides. The technique is called *trompe l'oeil*, an optical illusion of fake window frames, fake shutters, fake flowers on fake balconies.

It reminded me of another type of illusion: fiction. I knew nothing yet about the greatest illusion of all: the creation of the world.

The time of departure was approaching, I could feel it. When my casts came off, we would return to eternity, as we had silently agreed. I wanted to believe that eternity was just like the Riviera. But I sensed that for my husband it meant something completely different: an amorphous no-thing, a protean no-where. I knew He admired Schelling's conception of space as nothing real, as lacking energy and substance. As the form of things without their bonding force; the hypostasized without hypostasis.

During our walks, I liked to lean my head on His shoulder. A delightful miscellany of sights and sounds: the soft hiss of my husband's breath, the whoosh of waves, the patter of children's feet across a church courtyard, the clang of Sunday bells. The village came alive on Sundays: boys on bicycles gaggled at the wharf. Men and women strolled with their tiny dogs. And we sauntered, lingered, lost ourselves among the crowds. We frequented the open-air flea market and loved browsing through the messy heaps of heteroclite objects, like artefacts of lost civilizations: fur hats, medals, crystal decanter stoppers, umbrella stands, footstools. We did not touch the old books, the Polaroid cameras. Once, I said in jest: "How about I buy you a wristwatch and You buy me this fountain pen and inkwell?" "Not a chance," He replied flatly. That same day He bought me a large raffia beach bag and a small wallet. I got Him a pair of amber cufflinks.

He ended up using the wallet and raffia bag. He locked and unlocked the door to the house. He gave me painkillers, fed me, and helped me on with my nightgown at night. All I could do was walk and talk. My arms cradled under my chest, in the grey waterproof sling they'd given us at the hospital.

When we came across other couples our age, we greeted them with slight nods. Eventually, we became friendly with a couple who were also regulars on the Riviera. He wore a vest over his starched shirt, she a double string of pearls and red lipstick. They walked arm in arm, and whenever they saw us, they stopped to chat. They recommended restaurants, walks, a good hospital for the removal of my casts. God spoke their language; He translated every word.

One day, they told us they were retired schoolteachers. When they asked what we did, God replied vaguely, "Writers." Another time, they asked where we came from. He replied, "Savotia." Embarrassed, the teachers glanced at each other. They had not heard of the country. "Hardly surprising," He remarked. "Savotia has only just gained its independence." I asked Him how Had come up with that name. From savory," He said. "It thrives in sun-drenched, rocky terrain. Like you."

The closer to humanity He grew, the more urgent became our love. His elusiveness—the fact that His nature was always somehow beyond me—rendered our walks on the Riviera a deeper form of reconciliation.

As soon as the casts came off, we rented a motorbike. We'd point to a spot on the map and take to the road. The tourist season had not yet begun, and it was all ours: ports, museums, castles, churches, lanes. On the coastal roads, I clung to Him. Wind whistling, His hair lashing my face. Heart full.

In the afternoons, we played chess on a board we'd found at the market, its pieces carved from bone. He usually won. When He let me win, I'd pompously proclaim, "My knight takes Your queen." At night, I'd sink into the hollow of His shoulder and sleep serenely until morning. Despite His body's new substance and heft, I did not desire Him. At least not like that. He had made sacrifices for me, and I for Him. He was my world, the axis around which I revolved, my immaculate self-causation—*causa sui*. To embark on this journey with me, to suffer me clinging to Him, to walk at my side without asking for anything: it all meant that He, too, loved me.

We slept like that, without desire. Nestled one within the other, amorously sexless. Like the line in one of Neruda's sonnets, His hand upon my chest was mine.

OUR HOUSE WAS on the outskirts of town. We'd go down to the port to shop, eat fish, watch ships dropping anchor. God liked ships. Standing on the pier, He'd watch, enthralled by the life of the port: trawlers loading and unloading, fishermen at their longlines, men gesticulating next to the bollards.

Rarely did I get the chance to watch Him from afar. I picked through shell necklaces in tourist shops, my eyes not leaving Him for a second. To everyone else He was simply a man no longer in the first flush of youth: white mane combed back; bushy beard; thick grey eyebrows; serene, inscrutable eyes. To me He was a chameleon. Nut-brown from the sun, lips more prominent, nose thinner—feminine is how I would describe it. Don't misinterpret that comment: His gestures had acquired a feminine quality. His gait was like that of once-beautiful women: slow and with a deliberate stateliness, like the cargo ships He admired. You must know what I mean. When I could no longer abide the distance, I would careen into His arms.

"Ah, if only you would—"

"What?"

"If only we could go and live somewhere else—anywhere."

"You are quite mad," He would say, laughing. "How could that be possible."

These weren't our words. They were Emma and Rodolphe's in Flaubert's *Madame Bovary*.

I wouldn't stop there: "Be not afraid of life."

"We live as we dream—alone."

"It takes two to make an accident." Once again, others' words: Henry James, Joseph Conrad, F. Scott Fitzgerald.

It was no different when He started it: "You're not at all the same person."

"What! Have I changed for the worse?"

Nikolai and Natasha from *War and Peace*. Words buried deep within us.

THE BIBLE (THE table I rest on as I write to you in bed) is the only book we brought back to the House. On the last day, I found it in the drawer of my bedside table, and begged God to let me take it with me. Grudgingly, He agreed. A pencil was out of the question.

As usual, He could not resist a reproof: "One weeps not save when one is afraid, and that is why kings are tyrants."

And I, in an attempt to wring a drop of mercy from His heart:

"One paralyzes someone, cripples him, strips him of his unique characteristics, his thoughts, then his feelings, then deprives him of the instinct for self-preservation, then kicks him when he's down. No beast does that. The wolf doesn't kill a humiliated opponent, for he simply can't kill him. Did you know that? He's simply incapable of biting the throat stretched out to him."

We were still talking through books. He, the Marquis de Sade. I, Ingeborg Bachmann.

I laugh imagining the cleaner's face when she opened the door to our apartment after our departure. What did she do, I wonder, upon seeing thousands of books stacked to the ceiling? Did she scream? Did she call reception? Or did her shrieks summon the doctor and his assistant? I see them all crowded around our open door, astonished, hesitant. Taking pictures of the room, as if it were a crime scene. The arrival of police inspectors, a forensics team.

I wonder whether it occurred to them to turn our apartment into a shrine. I see the faithful kneeling amongst our books, praying to the hallowed Saint Fiction. Their path to salvation strewn with greedily devoured tomes, testaments to their prostration before the altar of human frailty. A new religion of impassioned acolytes, their backs turned on real life, capable of killing for their book.

As for us, we had become the books we read. We loved, quarreled, and reconciled borrowing word for word from novels, short stories, poems. We had absorbed more than we thought we had. We could even tell what lay in the future. It was written in the stars, as people say in talking about fate. That's because fate is an author.

You probably find me cold: I analyze as my heart beats, in the same breath. But I, too, might point to your coldness. I might contend that you keep reading only to see what will happen to me. This does not mean you are a bad person. You are curious, and your curiosity is my only hope whenever it occurs to me that one day, without warning, you might get up and leave.

ONE MORNING, WE visited the cathedral of the neighboring town. As black and white as a printed page, built on top of

Roman ruins, and famed for the relics of St. John the Baptist stored in a special urn. God was amused by the human ingenuity of it all: "Look at this memorial! You drop a coin in the slot and the entire thing lights up."

"Are those really his ashes?"

He shrugged. "As far as I know, the crusaders dug around in the Roman crypts and unearthed some bones."

"These aren't bones."

"No. They're ashes. Brought back from Myra in ancient Lycia. Apparently, the head is somewhere else."

"What do You know about it?"

"You want more fairytales?"

"No. I'm tired of lies." I took a seat on the back pew.

He sat down next to me. "You don't know the truth because there is no truth."

"Yes, there is."

"No, there isn't. Neither truth nor purpose."

"He shall call upon me, and I will answer Him."

"I did not write the psalm. Nor do I agree with that explanation."

"Give me another one then."

"There is no explanation because there is no mystery."

I got up and left the church without turning to look back. At times, I wanted to dig my nails in His face. To see if I would draw blood.

I REMEMBER THE voice echoing inside me: "Leave," it said, "escape while there's still time. Go somewhere far away. Run! What are you waiting for? One big leap and off you go: out of the world, off the map. Why should He be the one to disappear you at will? Why don't you disappear Him instead? How much longer are you going to tolerate His secrecy, His arrogance, in silence? 'There is no explanation because there is no mystery.' Does that answer satisfy you? And if not, what are you going to do about it? Are you going to let Him keep on dragging you from one place to the next? Or are you going to live your life with pride, as a fully realized individual? If the world scares you, then take to the mountains. Feed on wild

grasses, drink turtle blood. What are you waiting for? Life, the
freedom you dreamed about in books, beckon. Go on then: live!"
   I dashed along a back alley, ran down the steps that led in
the direction of the sea. Behind me stretched streets and lanes,
narrow paths among the rocks. I got lost in the maze of alleyways
and emerged on a busy main road. How wild was my heart's
delighted beat! I was tired of being good. Of appealing to God
and the genteel couples of the Riviera. Of mouthing pleasant-
ries with a smile, as if I knew the meaning of good manners. I
wanted to let loose, to misbehave, to act like a true devil. I did
something I had read about in books: I dashed across the coastal
highway even though the traffic light was green, dodging the
cars. Someone yelled a curse at me. A woman honked her horn.
I ignored them. Slumped over the promenade railing, gasping for
air, I stared all around me. I couldn't see our house anywhere. No
one was expecting me, I thought. Nor was I expecting anyone.
   All day, I walked without losing sight of the sea. I passed
villages familiar from our trips on the motorbike. Belfries jut-
ted up into the sky, cliffs plunged into the sea. In one village, I
stopped to drink water from a tap in a wall. I had no money for
food. Night found me clambering over rocks. At first, I thought
I would emulate those fasting hermits who hide themselves away
in caves. I didn't find a cave. But I did find a relatively comfort-
able rock. The night was warm. Hugging my knees, I fell asleep.
   Birds and the sun bathing my cheek woke me. The horizon
was on fire. I closed my eyes again to remember my dream: God's
kingdom was now a tourist destination. And there I was, God's
wife and accredited tour guide, sporting my name tag. I wandered
around, a tall glass in hand, regaling visitors with stories of life
with my husband. Whenever I raised my arm to point something
out, champagne spattered my wedding dress. Tourists were taking pictures with their cellphones. They wanted to know if God
used an alarm clock in the morning and brushed His teeth after
meals. In unison, they asked: "Does He swim in the lake? Does
He work out? What are His thoughts on the Second World War?"
A woman with yellow eyes started howling: "Enough already,
you're pulling our leg! We came to see God, not you!"

"I'm sorry," I replied. "God is dead. I am His widow. If you are weary of life's trials and tribulations and don't know where to turn, don't lose hope. My husband is waiting for you." They fell to their knees lamenting. "She's to blame!" screamed the yellow-eyed woman. "She killed Him! Punish her!" They stopped their weeping and wailing and turned on me, surrounded me, their eyes glowing. "She is bad, evil." "Punish her." And I, glass in hand, kept objecting, calmly, politely: "No, no, I'm good. Look how good I am! I represent God's vision of human kindness and grace! Look!" I started dancing, each pirouette taking me further and further from their midst. Beside our fence, where the Angels once played soccer, plunged the sheer cliffs of the Riviera. To escape the tourists, I climbed the rails and dived head first. I must have been planning to fly away. Instead, I fell, floating gently like a feather. Soon, I was going to land on a strange sea of frozen cement waves. But as I neared them, they changed into trompe l'oeil waves of paper. They swallowed me whole, but I easily bobbed back up to the surface. I swam all night in that origami universe.

I ought to have had a Plan B, but I didn't. I endured three days on the mountain. My tongue swollen, my eyelids withered. In fiction, escape always seems so easy. The nights are short, food is not terribly important, and the characters always encounter a life-changing someone or something. That was not the case for me.

I went down to the nearest village. With cupped hands, I gulped water from another roadside tap. Sitting on the sidewalk, I held out my hand, like a fictional beggar. Passersby dropped a few coins in my palm without looking at me. Enough to buy a sandwich and still have change. That's when I entered the first stationery store I found and bought a beautiful, perfectly sharpened 2B pencil. The kind we used to have at school.

I could not go on like that. I had been brought to my knees by despair, but also by something deeper: hunger. Bowing my head, I took the road of return.

ONCE, GOD WAS all alone, talking to Himself, conceiving of

Himself within Himself through Himself in order to see Himself thereby. For humans, this would spell schizophrenia, but for God it was the ground zero of joy. Nothing existed before God; He was the source of His own existence. Somewhere deep down in His primordial consciousness, He must have felt all His energies coming to the boil. A cosmic explosion in the making, a release of the immense power that was He. A deluge of life—yes. I don't remember which philosopher it was who said: "God is something more real than a merely moral world order and has entirely different and more vital motive forces in Himself than the desolate subtlety that the abstract idealist attribute to him."

But who cares what the philosophers say? What matters is what God says. That night—for it was night when I arrived back home—God was waiting for me on the balcony. I had prepared a speech for my return, but He did not let me speak. He did not even ask where I had been. As I already told you, He pulled the folded page out of his shirt pocket and read to me in His calm, clear voice.

Actually no, it didn't happen quite like that. First, I tore off my clothes and dashed to the shower. I scrubbed and scoured, put on my nightgown, and curled up under the sheets. He waited until I was comfortably settled and only then did He sit next to me and read from His page, as if we had left a conversation half finished: "I know my fate." He glanced at me to make sure I was listening, and continued: "One day my name will be associated with the memory of something tremendous—a crisis without equal on earth, the most profound collision of conscience." He talked until dawn.

I didn't interrupt—not even once. I lay there under the covers, listening to the strange story of Being unmade. I clung hungrily to every detail: the impunity of an existence that spans all eternity; the darkness of chaos and His tailspin into it; the cataclysms of Creation; the invention of light. I imagined a pure white expanse, like the paper I used to draw on as a child. And there was God, standing in the middle of it, inventing flowers for the bouquets of the future.

"But we don't know what God looks like."

"We'll find out soon enough."

I could hear, as clearly as could be, my mother's voice min-
gling with mine, there, in our kitchen. I was so young, but I
already knew. As you, too, know. What you expect from me is
a good story, not the truth, right? We already know the truth;
we feel it in our guts. We sense the primordial absence of matter
and the fate it holds in store for us. We are aware of the laws of
entropy. We have all witnessed the rotting of apples.

Every time we dream, we succumb to the memory of what
lies in store. Trundling wearily, we travel toward the nowhere
that stretches tantalizingly before us, its view constantly shifting
to keep us on our toes. Just like God, who planted incomplete
skeletons in Ethiopia, in its wake this nowhere seeds rivers and
barren valleys, islands, fantastic flora, and whispers "Come!" And
we go, pretending we don't know where we are heading. We conceive the inconceivable and then struggle all our lives to forget
by writing books, clipping our ever-growing nails, ploughing the
earth. We are nothing but the gymnastics of sentience, an elastic
dam, disorder. Explosions, feathers, dust, and here we are again,
disgorged into another history, onto a beach of strange pebbles.
If we ever meet, I want you to bring me one of those pebbles. It
will be our secret sign.

Now, back to our story. When the sun bloomed in the sky,
my husband rose from the bed and went to look out of the balcony door. Without turning to me, He said: "Time to pack your
things. We're leaving."

GOD IS ECCENTRIC, mysterious, dangerous. If He weren't God,
He would be a romantic hero. Byronic, melancholic, His head
in the clouds. A loner, holding out against society and its stifling
conventions. A true poet, transported by the spectacle of rain-
fall trickling down the midveins of leaves. Gloomily pondering
the ruins of civilization, the ancient columns of my country.
Beguiling to women because of His secret past. Appealing to
men because of His experience and wisdom. An object of fear
to children, who sense His disdain for fairytales.

If He were a writer, He would be Goethe. Or Keats. If
He were a book, He would be Chateaubriand's *René*. Like its

self-exiled protagonist, He might gaze at the Appalachians and say of His tribulations: "Absolute solitude, the vision of nature, soon plunged me into a state well-nigh impossible to describe. Without parents, without friends, alone on earth, so to speak, and not yet having loved, I was overwhelmed by the superabundance of life."

And if asked to describe the feeling of superabundance, His reply would surely be as evasive as René's: "The sounds that render passion in the void of a solitary heart resemble the murmurs the winds and water produce in the silence of a desert; one experiences them, but cannot describe them."

He is very much like René, who journeyed the world before returning to his homeland and his sister, Amelie (is that me, I wonder?). Secretly in love with him, the sister retires to a convent. Unlike Chateaubriand, however, God knows how to reconcile monastic cell and marriage bed. Oh, awesome indeed is His self-sufficiency! He says the word, and behold, the world is born. His words, like those of romantic heroes, are pure farce: "I feel that I love the monotony in the feelings of life, and, if I were still foolish enough to believe in happiness, I would seek it in an orderly existence."

It was to this orderly existence He demanded that we return. To the orderliness of eternity. He had already started changing. His body, its contours, were losing their definition, beginning to blur.

"But why? Why must it be like this?" I asked, my voice breaking.

He smiled sadly, wearily. "Because it is the only way."

"What about me?"

"You too will fade. Very gradually. Have faith."

I HAD BOUGHT a suitcase for our books. Now, without books, I used it for my belongings: dresses, beach towels, shawl, Buddha statue, aromatic candles, chessboard. On my knees, I pulled open the drawers of the bedside table. I found the Bible. I packed my earrings in a little bag; my shoes, in their canvas totes. I nestled the umbrella and the hairdryer among the clothes at the bottom of the suitcase.

"Where are you taking all that?" He asked. Seated on a folding chair on the balcony, He was watching me with empty eyes.

"What do you mean? I can't leave it here."

"Of course you can."

"What about our chessboard?"

"We don't need it."

"And the money?"

"Especially the money."

"Shall I take my dress off, too?"

"Now is not the time for jokes."

After His revelation, He resembled the fishermen who binge drink in the taverns along the wharf. He was in His own little world, ensconced in it so well that it was as if He had ceased to exist. So deep was His silence.

I closed the suitcase and shoved it in a corner, troubled by the conundrum it would pose to its finder. Squatting over the toilet, I buried the pencil in my vagina. Now, I too had a secret.

When I returned, He was in the same position, with His back to the room. I followed His eyes as they roved over the sea, the cliffs.

"Are you ready?" He turned to look at me. "Are you ready?" He repeated.

Heavy of heart, I nodded, clasping the Bible to my chest.

He told me to sit beside Him and close my eyes.

"No," I begged. "A little longer."

It was the height of summer. The world around us sparkled, a drawing engulfed in flames. I looked around me greedily, like a fictional character awaiting the executioner's bullet.

ANGELS, TALKING ALL at once, surrounded us. *Fhhtkrdxhgfxgfx.* God ignored them. After a while, they quietly withdrew. I envied them their submissiveness. Who were those strange beings that lived among us? Had they taken solitary walks with God in the Forest? Had they leaned against His shoulder? Had they said, "I love you?" Had they misbehaved with the Beasts, or had they patiently abided to the end, until it was finally time to join that grotesque nursery?

Then God vanished without trace. Even I don't know for how long. Without east or west; with neither calendar nor compass, how could I have known? The House, the clearing, immaculate and immutable as always. Manicured bushes, pristine trees, glimmering butterflies.

During that time, I spent my days in the Forest. Standing over the waters of the Lake, I pondered the irony of metaphor: Lake, the stillness of eternity. Every now and then, I'd fly, but the novelty had worn off. On the Riviera promenade, I had loved and trusted my husband; on the motorbike, I had clung to Him with all my strength. Now, barely skirting the tops of trees, I tried to rival His speed. What to do with His terrible Revelation? Creation, as He described it, was pure tyrannical decree. He had started the engine of cosmic ejaculation, and had brought forth all there is. Then, in the name of freedom, He had abandoned His progeny.

This is what I mulled over when I couldn't sleep at night. I hatched plans for my return to the world, for my betrayal of His secrets. I had to do something. To act using what I had to hand. Even if it was only a pencil. That's why I started writing this lengthy letter to you. Often, I scribbled a phrase I didn't want to forget in the margins: *rerum absentium concupiscentia*. What is desire if not the longing for things absent?

You are the thing absent. The very definition of excision. The void of your absence made me more inclined to forgive God (just as the void left by God's absence makes some people more inclined to love others). But His trust in me, too, was both courageous and naive, like the grand gestures one finds in fiction. What would I have done alone in the world? Without parents or companion, alone in a vast, dark room? Now that I think of it, that's a very good description of how I felt. And He knew. And He kept me close. My predicament is trivial in comparison to the ontological dimensions of my husband's. Yet I, too, was forever displaced from the world I knew. As for God's kingdom, I know too much to pass myself off as the innocent wife.

Yet innocent or guilty, I am still His wife. My place is here, at His side. He took care of me, educated me, gave me comfort and the world of books. I love Him and can finally say with certainty: I cannot live without Him. But if you love Him, I hear you say, why are you betraying His secret? I don't know. I simply cannot stop writing to you. Mine is merely a hand that holds a pencil.

GOD APPEARS IN the dining room. He sits, looks pensively at His plate. A shadow of Himself. I'm not exaggerating. I have never seen Him so absent from the body He once wore so naturally.

"What's wrong?"

No answer.

"Are you angry at me?"

"No," He replies miserably.

Somewhat insincerely, I say, "Patience. It will all work out."

A terrible thought occurs to me: What if He hasn't changed? What if I perceive Him differently because I'm the one who has changed? He had told me on the balcony: "You too will fade. Very gradually. Have faith."

I touch my skin. It still covers bone. But it is sheer and white. Like a sheet of paper.

TODAY I FEEL better. I even moved all my things into the laundry room, where I now write to you. Where are you? What are you doing? My only certainty is that you are not reading me. What a pity, since we are both at the same point in the story. Waiting to see what happens. Why can't I see you?

You are right: how could you possibly read what I'm writing as I write it? Unless you is me and I is you. It's the only way we will meet. Only God is capable of such feats: conceiving of Himself within Himself; revealing Himself unto Himself. For our kind, as I've said before, this spells schizophrenia. Is this, I wonder, the worst that might befall us? Madness? But, then again—remember? There is madness in solitude, but community in two.

Wait, there's someone at the door. Just a second.

IT'S MY HUSBAND. I open the door, step aside to let Him in. He stands on the threshold, peering at the room. "What a strange room. I don't understand why you shut yourself in here all day."

"I like it."

"There are no windows."

"I don't care."

"No, of course. You have fashioned your own and genuinely believe you have a view of the outside. But they're just trompe l'oeil windows."

"What do you mean?"

My husband's image disappears. Before my eyes, He turns into pure Aristotelian aether.

"Where are You? I can't see You."

"I see you. I am talking about the book you are writing."

I bow my head. "It's not a book. It is a letter that—"

"It is a book." His voice thunders in my head.

"Let me explain."

There's no need for me to explain anything, He says. He has been waiting for my fever to abate, for me to get up on my feet again. Now, it is my turn to wait. The Angels will call me to the Conference Room.

I WAIT TO be summoned. Pencil in hand. Now that He knows, there's no point in hiding. I write a couple of lines, get up, sit back down again. Clumps of my hair are falling out. I use a paper napkin to pick it up and throw it in the trash. My skin is peeling, flaking off. I'm afraid to look at myself. What am I saying? There are no mirrors here.

I drop the pencil and look at my hand: withered, dehydrated. You know the Francis Ponge poem about the orange? It tries in vain to return to its previous shape after being squeezed. Its seed, says the poet, is wood, branch, and leaf—the raison d'être of the fruit. Oh, poor Francis Ponge! You had no way of knowing the truth about the creation of the world.

THERE IS NO end, no beginning, God declares. Only constant repetition. He has no idea why I wrote those terrible things, how I came up with them.

"You told me," I repeat.

"What did I tell you? That the world began with a yellow flare? That I ran to hide in a cave with my tail between my legs?"

"You said that—"

He interrupts: "What you call nothing," He says, "is the absence of autonomous existence. The world comes into being only through complementarity. You've read Einstein. You've read Niels Bohr."

"Yes, but You said that we arrived at complementarity through—"

"Now is not the time for such talk," He says. "I remind you only that you are here of your own volition. Life's greatest gift is freedom. Are we agreed so far?"

"Yes," I say.

I cannot tell where His voice is coming from. It is disheartening to talk to Him in the absence of His physical presence. This is my first time in the Conference Room. I am at the head of the large, empty table, which stretches in front of me with the gleam of a freshly waxed floor. Angels are seated all around me. Silent and expressionless, they avoid my eyes. I warned you about their contrived, insincere attention.

For the duration of this trial I address you mentally. The Angels have taken my pencil, my paper. My Book (that's what God called it), is still being written, as long as I don't lose sight of you, as long as I continue narrating all that transpires.

One day, He found me in a bookstore, do I remember that?

"No," I say, "I don't remember."

In a big international bookstore, He repeats. I was standing, reading *Don Quixote*. Even though He disapproved, I put my foot down and bought the book. He warned me about the dangers of fiction. He asks if I remember what I replied.

"No," I say, "I don't remember."

I said that He fears fiction because it reminds Him of something He wants to forget: the creation of the world. We had a big fight in the bookstore. He repeated that, to a temperament like mine, there is nothing as seductive and dangerous as the false and foolish fancies of fiction.

He speaks in short sentences. As if I'm stupid.

He tells me that every day I brought bags of books to the apartment.

He says that I refused to go outside, to take walks with Him.

He says that He was worried about me and wished to see me joyful and carefree, like in the old days. As long as we were still in the world, however, He was powerless to intervene in my exercise of free will.

"Whereas now you can?" I ask.

He tells me that I piled books all over the apartment, building a platform of sorts from which one day I tripped and fell like Anna Karenina.

He tells me that in order to pull me out of the morbid world of fiction and help me remember what life truly was, He took me to a sun-drenched town by the sea.

He says that at first I seemed to be on the mend. Soon, however, He realized I was echoing sentences from the novels I read. I would point my finger at the replies He had to recite back to me.

He tells me that one day, in a cathedral, I had flown into a rage because He refused to confirm whether the ashes in a reliquary belonged to John the Baptist.

He says that shortly thereafter, I vanished.

He says that three days later, I returned to our room, much the worse for wear.

He says that I was ranting and raving about ultimate truth, about the deviations of the self, about oneself as other.

He says that the combination of fiction and my return to the world irrevocably damaged me.

He says that even when we returned to His kingdom, I wouldn't stop ranting and raving.

He says that the Angels found me in the Forest, my clothes in tatters, my hands full of splinters.

He says He read my book.

He says that what I've written is meaningless mumbo jumbo. And that if my aim was to infuriate Him or muddy the waters, I ought to know that I won't succeed.

He says that the answers I seek are non-existent; that all there is, is an open space of conjecture. A constantly shifting, protean space, like an earthquake zone. As unruly as the growth of wild brush. As elusive as the constant ebb and flow of the sea. That space, says God, is the human space. The space of doubt.

I say, "But You talked about faith."

He says, "That was the pre-condition for our life together, rather than the inherent human condition."

I say, "No, You never clearly stated that."

He says, "I gave you so many books to read."

I say, "Books are one thing and You are another."

He says, "Remember our conversations about religion?"

I say, "I don't mean philosophical discussions. I mean our day-to-day life together."

He says, "Our life together is defined by the world I created for us to live in together. You found it one-dimensional. All you were interested in was asking where the sun and moon had gone."

I say, "You cannot imagine the pain caused by the camouflage of mimicry: when a mock moon turns into mockery of the moon."

He says, "I'm sorry you misunderstood my intentions."

I say, "You never explained anything to me."

He says, "And you learned absolutely nothing from me."

I say, "I'm beginning to."

He says, "You have no idea what it means to be Godfearing. Don't you understand it is too late?"

I say, "How can it be too late, when time doesn't exist?"

He says, "Has it occurred to you that there are things far beyond you; things that you will never comprehend?"

I say, "No. Nothing is beyond my imagination."

He says, "That is precisely why we can't live together any more."

I say, "You don't mean that."

He says, "Yes, I do."

I tell Him I love Him, but that I find His logic oppressive.

He says He finds my imagination oppressive.

GOD'S ENTRANCE INTO the dining room is all flourish. There is no body, only a floating head that flickers before me like a candle flame. I must get used to this new look of His, suggestive as it is of decapitation. I mustn't make a quip about John the Baptist.

"Look, we are both getting blurry," I say. "We're beginning to look alike."

God does not reply.

"What is happening to me?" I ask. "I'm so white and one-dimensional."

Silently, He looks at me, eyes full of tenderness. He hesitates, then suddenly requests:

"Tell me that joke about Jonah again."

"It would have approached nearer to the idea of a miracle, if Jonah had swallowed the whale."

God's smile is pained. I wish I could smile. My mouth is too cramped.

I say, "Tell me what You're thinking."

He says He is thinking of Empedocles, a poet and magician who believed he had become a living God. He asks if that is what I aspire to.

"No, no, no, for God's sake! I'm your wife. Perhaps I didn't give the role its due respect, but I'm human. You know better than I what that means."

"Even so, you think that I don't know anything about humanity," He says. "That I don't understand it."

"You mean to say You do?"

A moment's silence. Then, He asks whether I believe that fiction has any bearing on life's ethical dilemmas.

I say, "Remember how upsetting You found that quip of George Bernard Shaw's?"

He says, "I don't like the theatre. It is a bad imitation of life."

I say, "Whereas I do not like life. It is a bad imitation of the theatre."

He asks which I love more, Him or fiction.

I ask, "What do you mean?"

He says, "Answer however you like."

I do not know what to say. I want to fall at His feet, but He no longer has any.

God's face looms nearer, as round and pale as the moon. "I

have come up with a plan," He declares. Getting straight to the point, He explains it in detail. He says He needs my consent. Without my heartfelt acceptance His proposal is meaningless. Acts are consequential only when freely embraced.

I ask Him whether He is finally going to tell me about the creation of the world.

He says that the only thing I need to know is that there was nothing instrumental about creation. It sprang from a primordial memory of freedom lost along the way.

I ask Him whether He will stay by my side.

He replies that He will, one way or another.

After further conversation, He asks whether I consent to His plan. His question is not really a question; it is a foregone conclusion.

I say, "Yes. I consent."

I want to hear it loud and clear. It's only His mouth now, intoning the words.

"I consent," I repeat. My voice is the merest whisper. My mouth is numb.

He smiles. How beautiful He is! Pure resplendence! A fount of light for a face; white beard atremble. The room quivers and vibrates around us. The walls turn silver like seawater under the sun.

"Then so be it," He mouths. A mouth as large as the one in my childhood dream. Opening wide, it swallows the entire room.

IT MAY SOUND like a lie: I am trapped in the Book. His plan was to banish me here; to relegate me to a life of endless wandering from page to page. After all, illusion and conjecture are what give my life meaning.

"Why so aggressive?" I asked Him.

"I don't know what aggression means," God replied. "You have been released from your role, from your promise of faith. You are free. With all my heart, I release you. You may write and rewrite, edit and revise your Book as you please. You may wander among its pages the way others wander around the rooms of their houses."

"Original—for a prison," I said.

No reply.

Through the dining room windows, I saw that night had fallen over God's kingdom with its customary suddenness.

"It's a book in the full physical sense," my husband continued, "like the books you read on our journey. There will even be pictures, if you want them. Just blink your eyes and images from the past will appear on the page."

"I'll still have eyes?" I wondered.

God said, "Don't pretend you don't understand. I am speaking metaphorically. Like moving an armchair around a room, you can change where you are in the narrative."

And so it is. In here, I do as I like with words. When I can no longer stand the stillness, my mind dives onto the page from a great height and I am undone. How prescient that dream about paper waves proved to be! The pallor of my hands, my peeling palms, the first stage in my metamorphosis to paper. Yes, the Book is real, concrete, but I am not. Not only because I am without body. It's actually a lot more complicated from an ontological perspective. The fact is, I simply do not know how to define my existence. Am I the Book's soul? The ghost of the person I used to be? Or am I merely the air wafting between pages as you leaf through them? You and I will never compare impressions. When I am here, you are elsewhere. And when you are here, you completely blot me out. My sentence is to exist only when you lay the Book aside. At least, that's what I believe. Like God, you too have the right to cast doubt on all I say.

Why did He ask my consent, when He had already started acting on me? Surreptitiously steering me in the direction of His plan? He steamrolled over me, squashed me as flat as a sheet of paper. And if a certain sharpness persists in my thinking, it is due only to the angularity of the four corners of my mind. He is sure to say: No, this is your doing! Your mad ravings again. You're the one who scurried off and hid yourself from the real world in that laundry room of yours. You're the one who willed your own metamorphosis into a book. You chose this cloister of words. They're what you wanted and now you have them aplenty, dear Mother Superior.

It was not words that trapped me, but original sin. My written revelations: the tree of knowledge. This is the doctrine to which I adhere: before I started writing life was an end in itself. Today, I fight for my salvation. How to contend with God? How to ask: Is a book that looks like a book really a book? Is a life that looks like life really life? God's trompe l'oeil is so realistic, that even I am blind to its deceptions. Am I? Am I not? What does it mean, I wonder, to be a living, breathing non-being?

HE IS RIGHT, repetition is everything. I am used to it, if you must know. I am diminished, inert, primed for the final stage of entropy. But how does one die inside a book? I forgot to ask God.

Occasionally, I am overwhelmed by claustrophobia. A suffocating weight, not of the page, but of all it contains. Words lend the paper life, they give it muscles, blood vessels, pumping arteries. More suffocating even than the Beasts that used to pounce before having their way with me. Desperate, I strip the surface to get out, like I once used to pick at Auntie's icon and, before that, at the Formica in the kitchen. How do I do that, you ask, without fingers, without nails? I do it with my mind. Lurking behind letters, I search for a crack through which to spy on the outside. I say "crack" like I once used to say "God is frowning." I have no idea whether the words I use correspond to reality. I know nothing of reality.

Another way out is more or less what my husband recommended: mentally, I dive into the paper and struggle to the surface dragging memories in my wake. I dedicate myself to a type of intellectual origami, cutting and pasting images and words. Where am I? How do I move? How do I write? With eyes and mouth? With mind and heart? The space I inhabit is the opposite of Schelling's conception of space as ungrounded ground, as immaterial materiality. In your language, I would say: I am light, weightless. I have great intensity and clarity. At the same time, I am trapped in the physical confines of this Book. Let's begin at the beginning: If I am that which substantiates, the Book is the product of that substantiation. It is a truly brilliant plan: The Book and I will never become one. We are condemned to be separate, two halves.

I remember this from when I used to live by God's side. Now, I am living it all over again with you. Have you noticed how children look at the elderly? How the elderly look at a child? Just like us. One comes, the other goes. Plagued by asynchronicity.

Any moment now, you will abandon me. Without the spell of illusion, we no longer speak the same language. For me, language is a black and white landscape. Sometimes, I hasten through it, vaulting from word to word. Sometimes, I linger, suspended over the void. Diacritical marks over vowels are a driving black rain, falling on me, within me. The empty spaces between paragraphs are white runways that make me dream of flight once more. I set myself a goal: any old goal, as Descartes once said, so long as you keep moving forward in the direction of your goal, at some point you will get out. In the confines of the Book, however, the discourse on method doesn't apply. Escape is an impossibility. We learned about it in school: $P(0) = 0$. There is zero chance of the impossible.

Don't let me keep you then. Far better you return home. Meet flesh-and-blood people who say, "What shitty weather!" or, "We'd love to have you over for dinner." Keep up with the latest government intrigue, the latest initiatives for saving the planet. Go then! Live your life. It is unutterably beautiful. I, who never really lived, tell you so. Never mind the cynics and their carping about catastrophe, sinking ships, suicide. Turn your face to the sun; let its radiance deliver you from reason. Run your fingers over the ridge of your collarbone—ah, the smoothness of skin, the hardness of bone! Lay your hand over your chest, over your heart, and say the words—don't be scared—really belt them out: I am alive! Three times like a prayer. God is great.

What's the very worst that could happen? A nightmare, possibly: you are God, or God's wife; You unfurl your wings to fly, but crash down to the earth instead. You let yourself fall into the void and are sucked into a maelstrom. You mop and mop endlessly, tirelessly; you try to break through the prison bars by beating your head against a wall. The fact of the matter is: You and I are bound forever. Perhaps one day, while your eyes rove opening seashores, my Book will appear before you—like an omen, like a shade risen from the dead—long after you have forgotten it. One of my sentences will spring to mind as if it were yours. You will not be wrong: we created it together.

I release you, Reader, with my blessing. Godspeed and may your actions result in good works, pleasing to God and man alike. Live your life in freedom and faith, and don't say that the two are incompatible, because we have demonstrated the opposite. Isn't that right? I will not forget your vague presence in my life. Your disbelief, your condescension, your compassion. Our collaboration helped me make my way through life, if what I am living is actually life. But no collaboration lasts forever. New wars are brewing, I can already see their wounds.

What will happen to me? As you can imagine, it does not depend on me. I've said what I had to say. Now, all I have written will be radically fragmented, as grotesquely disjointed as Angels' wings. Perhaps later it will be buffed, as smooth and shiny as the table in the Conference Room. Perhaps one day, God willing, my Book will wither, it will wane, its meaning will waft away in a puff of smoke, and I will break free of my prison. In the best-case scenario, the Book will self-actualize in its writing and will never bother anyone. It will be a book written for me alone; no one else will ever read it. Yes, an ethereal book, a book of ether.

My aim is to argue that it was never written. That you never read it. That it will not endure through the ages.

DEARLY BELOVED,

I write in the hope that You are listening—You, my one and only love. My feelings for my parents, my aunt, my classmates, the boy who waited to walk me home from school, were dress rehearsals for my love for You. I prowl round and round this nowhere like a tigress in her cage. The fact that you have put me here is not enough; I must learn to abide, to remain. And I do. Without complaint.

I deliberately bided my time before writing to You. My trials have whetted my love, helped me understand the pain I caused You. You offered me the world, and I asked for books instead— an endless supply of them. Fiction offered me an antidote to the atemporal world to which you brought me: it provided me with a sense of becoming. I read and wrote stories to find comfort, to forget. I now know what You meant by the natural inclination of things, about the meaninglessness of purpose. I stand here, still. Wearing your indifference to words and things.

How to prove my love to You? I comply with everything You asked of me while agonizing over the kind of expiation I think might please You. If I had knees, I would kneel and mutter Saint Bernard's prayer under my breath: "I proclaim my heart's desire for Him, supplicating His return." But I have neither joints nor nerves; neither a neck to support my head, nor a skull to encase my brain. I grieve for the wrists I broke during our journey. I grieve for my arms, my shoulders, my long hair. I miss the self I used to know. You have not shown me what to replace it with.

My love, as I wrote, I labored under the delusion that I was addressing someone else. As soon as I tried to banish that someone, I realized that that someone was me. So, yes, I accepted this indirect reflexivity, this symmetrical co-presence: in ceasing to read, I ceased to write. I don't know what the purpose of my soul is. I mean, if there is another purpose besides, of course, addressing You, dreaming You.

No, my mistake. I'm not dreaming You. In my dreams, I become one with You not because I see You, but because I can't. In the absence of Your image, I find Your primordial Self, static and still in absolute darkness. This is where I start: I fashion You from clay, then place You before me so that I may marvel at You. "Dream" is the wrong verb. I meant "create." I created You so that You would create me. You created me so that I would create You. And I am creating you, my Lord, I create You in every second of my struggle for meaning.

Sometimes, I think You are spying on me from behind fences, from behind bars. Then, I run without legs; I reach without arms; I scream without voice. Are You there? Do You still care about me? Ah, there You are! "Behold, He standeth behind our wall, He looketh forth at the windows, shewing Himself through the lattice." Is my imagination playing tricks on me again? I am sick, yes. Sickened by my obsession with learning the truth about

You. Hold me close, cure me of my human curiosity. Show me how to stop caring. I yearn for our House, our plane tree, the endless columns of the Forest. The butterflies, our flowers perpetually in full bloom, the placid waters of our Lake.

I renounce the Book. I don't want to write or escape, to contend or hypothesize. My only wish is to live quietly by Your side, a dog at Your feet, "for I am sick of love." Where is the city through which I might roam, like in our beloved poem? Where are the streets and the piazzas where I might ask: "Saw ye Him whom my soul loveth?" So I ask You directly, You who thrive on asymmetrical co-presence: Do You perchance see Yourself within Yourself, by means of Yourself, having a change of heart and gradually taking me back in?

Will You forgive me, my love? Will You take me back? I will wait as long as is necessary. "I adjure You that You not stir up or awaken love until it pleases."

Oh, Lord, why did You abandon me? This is worse than hell. Alone in the middle of nowhere, without walls against which to beat my head. What am I saying? If only I had a head, even if only to beat it against nothingness.

What am I supposed to do with words? They are the currency of another era, another world. Again, this awful asynchronicity between the tools You gave me and what I can do with them. Was Your point to show me the pointlessness of words severed from meaning? Was it to rip my tongue out by the root, to chop it to bits with a hoe? I have learned my lesson. Better to be at Your side and live in doubt than to have answers and be without You.

Let me tell it exactly the way I feel it: At first you disappeared in order to think up the best, the most difficult punishment in the world. Then you imprisoned me in the Book. You transformed me into an antecedent of our relationship, into the eternal unreliable narrator. Must I live within this story until Your truth is revealed? Where on earth is Your truth hidden? No matter which stone I turn, all I reveal is Your silence.

I'm sorry I misbehaved. It is a hard punishment indeed not to be able to eat or walk by Your side, not to be able to play a game of chess with You. Talk to me. Without You my words build a windowless house, a river that runs dry. I sit here, in the great nowhere, asking and answering questions all by myself. That's exactly what I did when I wrote the Book, You will say. That's right, I need a theory to live by. Your mind is great and orderly; capable of apprehending entire worlds of theses and antitheses. My brain is smaller than a fist—I mean, it used to be. I do not understand anything. I cannot tell if I swallowed the Book, or if the Book swallowed me.

You still deem me ungodly? Can't You see I have abandoned everything for You? Other people, the material world, my very self? What else do You need in order to believe me?

Please, I beg You, take me away from here. I will do whatever You want.

SHALL I TELL a joke? The living are the dead on holiday! How did I think that up? I must have read it somewhere. I have my books; over time I have learned to dive in and fish things out. You know what bliss means to me? To suspend all disbelief and live inside a story. Oh, why did I renounce reading and writing for so long? It wasn't only to prove my capitulation to You. No. It is on the doorstep of fiction that I lay all that went wrong between us. But was it truly wrong? Perhaps vice is actually the only path to virtue. Perhaps I should sing every day like a Sunday. Fiction is my religion. I pray without hands, read without eyes or mouth, conceive and imagine without the synapses of a brain. I sing Myself. And I am through with You.

God, you are heartless—the brute heart of a brute like You. You never loved me for what I am. In my earlier letters, my only thought was what would become of me. Now, I don't give a damn. It is intoxicating, at times. A habit like any other. Like that old habit of allowing someone to tell you what to do and how to do it, spurred both by the bright blue smile of approval and the boot in the face of censure. But now I'm tired and I'm through. I'm finally through with You.

Now, hear My story the way I want to tell it. Do You remember how to turn the pages of this book, or do I need to remind

You: "long hair twisted into a braid, skin covered in freckles, lips forced into an awkward smile whenever someone addressed me. I was the kind of girl who didn't want to displease anyone ever; who thirsted for constraints, for trials and tribulations." You took me from my home—kidnapped me, as a matter of fact—because You needed someone to walk by Your side. When You tired of my unripe mind, You began feeding me books. You became my mentor. Appearing out of the blue whenever You felt like it; asking whatever You wanted; never answering any question. Deep down, You are no different than the rest. The hordes who contend that woman came from Adam's rib, like an Angel wing. The Angel in the house, a prize trophy, a garden fountain. Water flowing only to quench Your thirst.

You demanded that I live outside time; You denied me all the pleasures of the flesh. Were You shocked when You read about the Beasts? Yet it was You who was the first to take advantage of me. You plucked me out of society as if I were a weed, one sharp tug and out I came by the roots. And here I am. I have no idea what is going on in the world, who is at war with whom. When I fell ill, You did me the favor of returning to the world with me. But even then, Your magnanimity was purely gestural, devoid of true understanding. You took me to a foreign land, a place of Your choosing. What did You expect? That I would get used to it? That everything would turn out to be fun and games? One book led to another. I discovered the only medicine for my pain: writing. What were You afraid of? That I would learn to lie? It's within those lies that You and I built our lives. Without lies, we would not exist.

I have made an important discovery, hit the mother lode, as they say. Irony has blown a gaping hole between me and the ideal Self I sought so eagerly. You wield irony better than anyone, but You do not feel its sting. Please forgive me this indiscretion: Your main problem is Your unbearable solemnity. And if indeed You are the ultimate frontier— again, please forgive me—You are also the very definition of contradiction. Shut up in Your Study, You hold forth on life, on creation, as if poring over a list of great works, as if grading a research paper. You cannot pull the wool over my eyes: You're an academic, a supervisor. You collect lost philosophers on the sterile shelves of Your ivory tower, where no one has ever let their hair down.

You won't get away with it no matter where You are. The same as I, You, too, will wander without rest, struggling to find meaning. In the end, this is what makes us equals, a genuine couple. I take back everything I wrote in my last letter: Better to have answers and live without You than to remain beside You and live in doubt.

In fact, I'm starting to like it here. I re-invent our story over and over again. This is my version: I revise therefore I am. Shall I remind you of the quote from Musil that I like so much? "God does not really mean the world literally; it is a metaphor, an analogy, a figure of speech that He has to resort to for some reason or other, and it never satisfies Him, of course. We are not supposed to take Him at his word, it is we ourselves who must come up with the answer for the riddle He sets us."

So here is what I came up with: I am putting You, too, inside the Book. Making You something more than words. Turning You into paper, glue, printer's ink. In this version of the story, You do not punish me. You take me straight to eternity, where You and I live together inside the Book forever. This is the reading I prefer. To me You are the ultimate frontier, my one and only conclusive idea. I love You stubbornly, desperately. In my mind, You *are* my childhood drawing: there You are, in the middle of a white page; and there am I, my pencil gliding over paper as I work on the bouquet You will later give me. And there is Mother, behind me, asking me, in the infinitude of time:

"What are you drawing?"

"God."

"But we don't know what God looks like."

"We will soon enough."

In case You haven't figured it out, I am writing a farewell letter. Even though You and I will never part. In the Library, I read about how entangled photons continue to communicate with each other instantaneously even when very far apart. My identification with You is absolute. When I get angry at You, I am angry at myself. When I am overcome with love for You, I come to terms with something imperishable within me.

Farewell, my Lord. If I must stay here until matter and anti-matter cancel each other out, then so be it. The strange workings of light and matter, the instability of quantum electrodynamics, has the Universe roiling with scattering particles, and there I am among them, a yellow paper flare tearing through the chaos, sparking once more Your dreams of a world of light and action.

If I were an army, we would now be discussing retreat. But is an army of one possible? And how does such an army retreat?

I keep circling around something without a name. What will be, will be. No matter what, I will face it with serenity and indifference. If I cease to resist, the thing I fear will finally reveal *its* face. I see it now clear as day: God and death make the same demand of me: to write my final sentence and surrender, to accept that the end of the Book means the end of my world.

There must be another world for me. Or many worlds. In the geometry of spacetime there are debates about the possibility of existence in multiple spaces simultaneously. Perhaps that is the answer. To use different ways of looking at what approaches, not head-on but aslant, from a multitude of perspectives. As if soaring to great heights. As if falling hard and fast.

How to give the Book the form of a helix, an ascending spiral coiling into infinity. I need an orbit. If I find it, my story will continue to twist and fold interminably, to rotate, to revolve around itself forever.

Good Lord, You are right. The answer is repetition. It is, in fact, much simpler than I imagined.

It may sound like a lie: I am His wife. We married ages ago. He asked for my hand and I said yes. Sometimes, not even I can quite believe all the things I have lived, first without Him, then by His side. I never imagined my life like this.